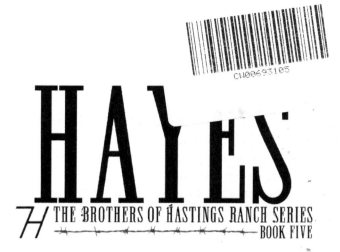

HAYES

THE BROTHERS OF HASTINGS RANCH SERIES
BOOK FIVE

By Katharine E. Hamilton

ISBN-13: 978-1-7358125-6-4

Hayes

www.katharinehamilton.com

Cover Design by Kerry Prater.

To Tulip.
Yes, that's my dog. My faithful, fifteen-year-old Chihuahua. Like Hayes with his horses, I find Tulip to be one of my best friends. We've lived a lot of life together, and the little diva keeps on truckin'.

Acknowledgments

Thank you to my family. It's been fun to write a series both sides of my family can relate to. Ranching and farming has been in my blood since I was a kid, and I married into the ranching realm. I wouldn't have it any other way.

Thank you to my editor, Lauren Hanson. We powered through some tough events while Hayes was underway, and I'm thankful we can be friends as well as work buddies.

My cover designer, Kerry Prater, for giving me one of my most favorite covers yet.

And my wonderful beta team, who continually have my back and spoil me with their support. Thank you.

H

Chapter One

He'd scrubbed the three largest water troughs in the outside pens and had swapped out clean water and feed buckets in the stalls. Now, all Hayes Hastings had to do was scrub the dirty buckets, let them dry out in the sun, and then place them in the storage closet in the barn. It wasn't his favorite work when it came to taking care of the horses. In fact, the last few months, he'd paid a couple of kids from church to come out and do the scrubbing. But this time, Hayes rolled up his sleeves and tackled the job himself. He didn't mind the tedious and wet work, and sometimes he wanted to do it himself to make sure the job was completed to his standards. And after a few months of distracted teens taking on the task, the buckets needed a good deep cleaning and sanitizing, Hayes style. He was particular when it came to the care of his horses.

His stables currently housed 12 horses of various ages and stages. Most of them were for him and his brothers to work cattle, but he had a few he'd been working with and training for other riders, especially a foul-tempered bronc that'd been giving him a hard time the last several weeks. But time was all Hayes needed. A little more time with the horse, working with him, teaching him to trust... rescue horses tended to take a bit of extra time to train. Not only were their bodies typically wounded and abused, but so were their spirits, and Hayes had been around horses enough over the span of his life to know that a horse's spirit is the most important attribute. So, he'd take time with the bronc, treating him tenderly but firm, giving the horse a steady, strong, and trustworthy presence that would influence his behavior. Time. He'd acquired the horse over five months ago, had his friend Alice, the local veterinarian, look him over, and then set about getting the young bronc used to the stables and being around other horses. He'd yet to have a saddle on his back, but progress had been made with a blanket two days in a row. And Hayes knew it was only a matter of time when he'd be able to climb aboard, saddle up, and start working on simple commands.

The crunch of rocks under shoes had Hayes looking up to see a timid Julia McComas walking towards him. He turned off the water hose and smiled at his future sister-in-law. "Well, hey there, Julia."

"You've been busy." She nodded towards the soggy ground, the empty buckets, and the sparkling troughs full of water that a few of the horses gathered around.

"Cleaning day."

"Looks like it." She slowly reached a hand through the fence to rub his oldest brother Graham's horse on the neck. She'd been scared of the horses the last few months due to almost being thrown off a scared mare. But Julia was determined to conquer that fear, not only for herself, but for Graham's sake as well. She wanted to be able to ride around the ranch with him, feeling comfortable in a saddle. So she came out once a day, sometimes in the morning, sometimes in the evening, but every day, to be around the horses.

"I have a favor to ask you, Hayes."

"Name it." He turned the hose back on and continued his scrubbing, Julia picking up a steel wool sponge and jumping into the work alongside him, still dressed in her scrubs from working at the vet clinic with Alice for the day. She worked some of the algae off the interior of the bucket and let Hayes add a little more water to help her along.

"So, I bought my dress."

"Oh yeah?" He glanced up and then paused. "Wait, *the* dress? As in the *dress* dress? Your wedding dress?"

She beamed. "Yep."

"Wow. Congrats."

"Thanks. That was a process, let me tell you," she laughed. "So many women, so many opinions. I finally just tried one on I liked and bam. That was it."

"I'm glad you found one. You going to give me a sneak peek? Is that what you need?" His eyes danced at the thought of seeing her in her dress and having to keep that a secret from Graham.

She chuckled. "No, but that's sweet that you'd be willing." She handed him the bucket for him to give it a rinse and then add a little more water for her to continue scrubbing it. He liked that Julia was the type of woman who had to keep her hands busy. Though she wasn't raised on a ranch, she understood the value of hard work and the constant need to keep things up. Her actions were mindless, natural, and she fit right in with his family. He was thankful Graham had found a woman who'd love his stubbornness and his lifestyle. "I'm to have bridal portraits in a week or so, and I was wondering if I could have some taken with Trisket. Do you think that'd be possible? She won't get spooked?"

"I think that's a great idea. Trisket's a good gal. She'll handle it all just fine; may even perk up at the extra attention," Hayes assured her.
"Would you mind helping?"

"Not at all. There are two things that touch a man's heart, Jewels. One, a woman who can cook, and two, a woman who loves a man's horse. I think Graham will be one happy man to have a photo of you with his beloved horse."

"I thought it might be special too." She blushed at the idea.

"Then consider it done. Just let me know the day and time and I'll have Trisket all gussied up for you."

"Thanks." She finished scrubbing the bucket. "Oh, and could you keep it a secret from Graham? I don't want him to know about it."

"My lips are sealed."

"You're the best, thank you."

"The *best*?" Lawrence's voice drifted over to them as he waltzed up carrying his saddle. "Why, Jewels, I'm offended."

She laughed. "All in the shadow of you, dear Lawrence."

"That's what I thought." He puffed out his chest and wriggled his eyebrows towards his brother. "What brings you out to the stables? You finally ready to run away with me?" He shook his head, disappointed. "You would wait until I ask another woman to marry me."

Hayes rolled his eyes as Julia giggled. "Something like that, though don't tell Ruby or Graham."

Lawrence winked at her as he walked into the tack room and placed his saddle on one of the rests, swapping it for a different one, and walked back out.

"Well, I will let you two get back to finishing up. I've got to start supper up at the house. Thanks again, Hayes."

"No problem."

"And as soon as I get everyone scheduled, I will let you know when."

"Sounds like a plan." He and Lawrence watched as she walked back towards Graham's house, stopping briefly to pluck a blade of grass to twiddle with on her way.

"Every time I look at her, I just don't know how Graham managed to snag her." Lawrence reached for the bucket she'd finished and started drying it with a towel without being asked.

"She's good for him, that's for sure."

"Agreed. What was she wanting?"
"I'm not supposed to say."

"To me?"

"Well, to Graham. But you can't keep a secret, so yeah, you either."

"I can keep a secret, especially from Graham."

Hayes looked doubtfully up at his brother.

"When it's important," Lawrence amended.

"She's wanting to take some bridal portraits with Trisket."

Lawrence gave a low whistle. "That'll earn some points there."

"Yep. She wants it to be a surprise for Graham. So don't say anything."

"I won't. That's big for our Jewels to even want to be around the horses, so I know it's a big deal to have her picture taken with one. In her wedding dress to boot. Ooooh I'm totally coming to help you when that goes down so I can get a sneak peek."

Hayes smirked. "I think I'll have an entire stable full of Hastings men hoping to catch a glimpse."

"We'll give Cal the duty of keeping Graham busy."

"Good call."

"You almost done with all that?" Lawrence pointed at the buckets. "Or am I riding alone today?"

"You're on your own. I've finished this but I want to clean out each of the stalls."

"You already mucked them this morning," Lawrence pointed out.

"Deep clean. They need a good thorough cleaning and that's what I plan to do today."

"Suit yourself. I'm going to enjoy this beautiful day atop my horse and avoiding Graham." Lawrence grinned.

"Good luck with that." Hayes wished his brother well with a wave as Lawrence hoisted himself into his saddle and clicked his reins.

"Have a little fun today," Lawrence suggested, guiding his horse towards open pasture.

∞

"So, there I was, sitting at the table with this delicious meal in front of me and absolutely no date."

"He never showed up?" Alejandra Garcia snipped the tips of the woman's hair with freshly sharpened sheers as she brushed a comb down to level the strands and snip again.

"Nope. Never showed. I mean, who does that?" Rachel Lewis continued her rant, and Ally sighed on her behalf for the unfortunate bad date.

"Good men are hard to find these days," Mrs. Cybil Richards called from across the salon, eavesdropping on their conversation.

"I will second that," Rachel agreed.

"I disagree." Alice Wilkenson's voice drifted from two chairs over as Sandy trimmed the split ends off her blonde hair. "You just have to know where to look."

"Alice Wilkenson," Rachel's voice dripped with annoyance as she glanced up at Ally in the mirror before narrowing her gaze on the veterinarian draped in a black cape and studying her reflection. "not all of us can just claim a Hastings as our own."

"There's plenty of them," Mrs. Cybil chuckled as Alice nodded in agreement. "And all of them are easy on the eyes, just like their grandpa was."

Alice grinned. "That they are."

"Speaking of the Hastings," Rachel's eyes sparked at the possible scoop of fresh gossip. "I hear Graham Hastings has completely been turned upside down by your friend from Santa Fe."

"He has," Alice admitted. "He's still the same old Graham, though Julia has softened him a twinge."

"I always thought he was the best looking," Rachel commented.

Ally, not knowing the Hastings family, just worked quietly on Rachel's hair and listened. That's what most people needed in a hairdresser: a good listener. She listened to their rants, vent sessions, or even shared in exciting life events with an open ear and friendly smile. She felt the eyes of the vet upon her, and she offered a polite nod before unclipping the next layer of Rachel's hair.

"I beg to differ," Alice smirked. "My Cal is pretty on point in the looks department."

Cybil laughed. "Calvin Hastings is a sweetheart. I just love how he holds the door open for me at church."

"Still, there's always been something intriguing about Graham. I think it's because he plays hard to get."

"He doesn't *play* anything," Alice corrected.

"You know what I mean," Rachel continued. "He's all broody and moody, but his face—" she fanned herself. "It only makes him more attractive."

"I'll be sure to let Julia know you approve of her choice," Alice replied sarcastically, and Ally detected a hint of disdain in her tone as well.

Rachel looked at Ally. "What about you, Alejandra? What do you think of the Hastings brothers?"

"I don't know them." Ally tilted Rachel's head forward as she tugged on the ends of her hair to make sure it was even across the back.

"You've never met a Hastings?" Rachel asked, flabbergasted at such a thought.

"Can't say I've had the privilege."

"How long have you lived here?" Rachel asked.

"Two years."

"Two years and you've never stumbled across a Hastings?" She shook her head in sympathy.

Ally shrugged her shoulders and continued her work, handing a mirror to Rachel so she could survey the back of her hair.

"Looks good." Rachel handed the mirror back and waited as Ally removed the cape and shook the excess hair onto the floor before walking towards the register. Ally followed her, accepted her payment and tip, and waited as Rachel turned one last look at Alice Wilkenson. "Tell the Hastings crew I said hello, Alice. And if you can ever convince any of the single ones to come to Sheffield more often, feel free to give them my number." She exited before Alice could hop out of her chair and ring her neck. At least, that's what it looked like she was about to do.

Sandy's cell phone rang on her worktable, and she glanced at the caller id. "Oh no. Sorry, Al, I've got to take this." She answered, and her face fell. "Yes, yes, yes, I'll be there in a few minutes." She hung up and looked regrettably in the mirror at Alice. "That was the school. Johnny's in the principal's office. Again."

Ally walked back towards her workstation and began sweeping Rachel's hair off the floor and straightening her tools and styling wands.

"Mind if Ally finishes you up?" Sandy asked.

Alice shrugged in indifference. "A haircut is a haircut."

"Ally, do you mind?" Sandy asked.

"Not at all." Ally smiled in reassurance as Sandy helped Alice over to Ally's styling chair and resituated her cape before snatching her purse out of a cabinet at her own station and hurrying to the door. "Just a trim, right?" Ally asked.

"Trim, cut, it's whatever you want to do. I'm not really picky about my hair as long as I'm able to pull it up into a ponytail."

"Alright." Ally smiled as she began evaluating Alice's hair and what work Sandy had accomplished up to that point. "Want a few layers?"

"Sure." Again, Alice seemed to not care, and Ally took that as a good sign, though a little intimidating. Most women knew exactly what they wanted or had a picture of what they wanted, so to have free rein was a rare opportunity. Alice had thick hair, and a few layers would add depth without fuss, and maybe she'd like it enough to spread the word about Ally's skill. Ally needed more customers. She was barely making enough to keep her booth at the salon, and though she'd been in Sheffield for two years, she'd only been at Sandy's salon for three months. She had a few clients she'd brought with her, but mostly, she was starting from scratch. She needed clients.

"So, you're new here at Sandy's, huh?" Alice asked.

"Sort of. Been here a few months."

"Well, I only come in like once a year for a haircut, so a few months is pretty new. How do you like it?"

"It's great." Ally smiled as she began running her comb through Alice's hair.

Alice nodded to a picture on the mirror in front of her. "That your little girl?"

"Yes. Ava."

"Cute. How old is she?"

"She's four, going on thirty."

Alice laughed. "Sounds like my kind of kid."

"She's pretty great." Ally walked to Alice's left side and continued clipping a new layer into the thick blonde strands.

Alice's phone dinged and she glanced at the text and sighed. "Oh Lord."

"Everything okay?" Ally asked, pausing a moment to make sure Alice did not need to suddenly leave for a pet call or emergency.

"Oh yeah, it's just my friend, Julia."

"The woman who swept Graham Hastings off his feet?" Ally asked.

"You were actually listening?"

Ally laughed. "It's part of the job."

"Well, yes, it is that woman. And that woman is about to drive me crazy," Alice continued. "In a good way. She had it in her head to convince Hayes to help her with Graham's horse for bridal portraits."

"And who is Hayes?" Ally asked.

"Oh, right, you don't know them. He's one of Graham's younger brothers. Great with horses. Anyway, Julia's scared of horses due to an incident a few months ago, but she wants bridal portraits taken with Graham's horse because up until Julia, Trisket was the only woman in his life that could stand him."

Ally grinned. "Sounds like a sweet idea."

"Oh, it will definitely make Graham fall even more in love with her, if that's possible. But now she wants me to recommend a makeup artist and stylist who'd be willing to come to the ranch on that day for the photo session. Do I look like I know a makeup artist?" Alice pointed to her unpainted face and rolled her eyes.

Ally straightened and met Alice's gaze in the mirror.

Alice perked up at the lightbulb that seemed to ignite from within Ally. "Wait... do you know how to do makeup?"

"I do, actually."

"Would you be up for it?"

Ally hesitated a moment. "Bridal portraits are a big deal. She'd most likely want me to do a test sitting first, sample a couple of looks before she decides."

Alice waved her hand. "Trust me, Julia will be easy."

Ally knew women who requested makeup artistry were anything but easy.

"How about you come to the ranch on Friday for a test run? I know it's a drive, but if you're willing to cut seven unruly cowboys' hair and maybe do a "test run" on Julia's face, maybe it'd be worth it?"

Ally's eyes flashed to Ava's photo. She didn't have childcare on Fridays, so she didn't work in the salon on those days.

"You can bring your daughter," Alice invited. "She won't be in the way or a nuisance. If anything, she'll force the boys to behave."

"Oh, well..."

"If you're fully booked for Friday, maybe we could aim for next week some time."

"No, Friday is fine. I'm open on Fridays." Seven haircuts and a makeup session would be a huge blessing, but Ally didn't want to seem too eager.

"You're receiving an invite to the Hastings Ranch," Cybil's voice drifted towards them. "Honey, take it." She winked at Alice before standing and following her hairdresser towards the cash register, her aged hand patting her new perm.

"Well, if you think they'd like to have their haircut, I'll be there. What time?"

"Morning okay? Like maybe nine? That gives the guys time to knock out a few things while it's still cool."

"Sure."

Alice smiled, and texted in her phone. "Julia's going to be pumped."

A responding ding had Alice holding up her phone for Ally to read the message. A small dancing figure did a happy jig on the screen and she grinned. "Hastings Ranch it is, then." Ally finished Alice's hair and gave it an extra styling since the vet was headed home for the day and anticipating a meet up with her own boyfriend, Calvin Hastings.

Pleased with the day's events, Ally wrote Hastings on Friday's open slot in her appointment book before gathering her purse and heading to pick up Ava from daycare. Seven haircuts on the books. Seven more potential clients. Today was a good day.

∞

"I don't need a haircut," Lawrence complained, and had Alice, Julia, Annie, and Ruby all eyeing him with doubtful expressions as they all sat and crowded the porch of the small guest house on the 7H Ranch. "What?" he asked. "I don't."

"Lawrence Dean, stop your whinin'," Annie, their life-long friend and surrogate mother, ordered. "You're startin' to look like one of those yuppy, wannabe hippies. You'll get your haircut, and you'll do it with a smile."

Lawrence, though not at all desiring to sit still long enough for a haircut, hid his smile as he attempted to rile Annie up even further. "Now, Annie—"

"Don't you 'Annie' me, boy. You'll do as I say. Respect the elderly," she added for more effect, and he chuckled, pulling her into a tight hug that lifted her off her feet.

"Now, where is Graham?" Annie looked at the clock as Lawrence set her back on her feet. "He's first."

"Why does he get to go first?" Seth, the youngest brother asked. "I'm the one that has to work the garden today. By myself. In the hot sun."

"Whine, whine, whine, whine, whine, whine, whine." Annie shook her head in exasperation. "You boys are going to wear me out."

"Now, Alice, when does the lovely Alejandra arrive?"

"She'll be here at nine."

"Alejandra." Clint rolled the name off his tongue with a wolfish smile. "I like it."

"And you'll behave yourself," Annie warned him. "You boys have had enough practice around beautiful women now that you should all be on your best behavior and know how to act."

"Speaking of beautiful women," Clint looked to Ruby. "you ditch the diner and leave Kara in charge, or will she be coming out?"

"She's running the diner," Ruby reported.

"That's a shame. Though I guess I don't have to go and shower now."

"If you only shower when Kara's around, that sure explains a lot." Alice curled her nose at him, and he playfully shoved her shoulder.

"You should be showerin' regardless of Kara's presence," Annie told him. "And for all our sakes." She waved him aside as she shifted the chair in front of the window that would serve as the mirror and workstation for the hairdresser.

"And why are you all of a sudden so interested in Kara?" Alice asked. "Don't you leave for New Mexico soon?"

Clint shrugged. "I can appreciate a pretty woman, can't I?"

"You can." Julia's voice snapped everyone's attention her direction as she struggled to carry a side table out of the guest house. "Show your appreciation to the hairdresser by setting this up by the chair over there, please." Clint tapped his cowboy hat, hopped off the porch railing, and lifted the table with ease and carried it to where Julia directed.

A small SUV began driving up the main entry and everyone's heads turned as Alejandra pulled to a stop in front of Graham's house. She opened her door and then immediately opened the passenger door behind her to unbuckle her daughter from her car seat. Alice hopped to her feet off the front steps at the guest house and walked over. "Hey! I see you found it okay."

Alejandra looked up with a smile as Ava, her daughter, sized Alice up in one sweeping look. "I did. It wasn't that bad of a dri—" Her words were interrupted by the pounding of hooves and hollers as Graham and Hayes raced their horses up from the neighboring pasture. Hayes, a horse length ahead of Graham, pulled to a halt in front of the main house as Graham did the same seconds behind him.

"And I win." Hayes held a fist up in victory, breathless from the hard ride, as Graham just shook his head and dismounted. He paused as he noticed the unfamiliar vehicle in front of his house and the woman and child he'd never seen before. Hayes had just unsaddled himself when a small squeal had him turning and finding a small girl running in his direction. Her hand was grabbed by the woman behind her, he assumed her mother, as the little girl struggled against the hold. He wrapped his reins around a hitching post and knelt to his knees in front of her. "Hi there." He flashed a friendly smile, and the little girl hid partially behind her mother's hand. "You like horses?" The little girl nodded. "You do?" His face lifted in genuine pleasure. "Well, did you know that Flash is the fastest horse to ever walk the planet?"

Her eyes widened as they took in his black horse eating lazily at the grass around his hooves. "Even beat ol' Trisket there." He nodded towards Graham's horse. "And Trisket is known for being fast."

"Is he nice?" The little girl's voice, soft and uncertain as she longingly gazed at Flash, had Hayes' smile widening.

"He's the best. He's mine. I trained him myself to be nice to pretty little girls. Wanna meet him?" He looked up at the mother, her eyes hesitant and watchful.

"Oh, can I, Momma? Please?" the little girl begged, her confidence returning as she tugged her mother's hand.

"I-I'm not sure, Ava."

"Oh, she'll be fine," Alice assured her. "Hayes, the horse whisperer, will see to that."

Alejandra looked to Hayes and he removed his dirty cowboy hat, his face already covered in a thin coating of dirt and sweat from his morning's work. He extended a hand to her, meeting dark wary eyes that tugged at him in a peculiar way. "Hayes Hastings, ma'am."

She nervously shook his hand and quickly released it. "Alejandra Garcia."

"And who is this?" he asked, kneeling in front of her daughter.

"Ava Garcia," the little girl replied, pumping his hand with enthusiasm. "I'm your friend."

Hayes's brows perked. "Are you? Well, I like the sound of that. I'm always looking for new friends."

His comment pleased the little girl as she looked up once more at her mother. "Can I pet his horse, Momma? I pet it?"

"Maybe just real quick, but then Momma's got to get to work, and you have your colors." She held up a small backpack full of childish activities to occupy the girl.

Ava squealed as she accepted Hayes's free hand and he led her towards his horse. He lifted her up on his side and showed her how to brush her hand down Flash's snout and cheek. Her eyes held pure wonder and thrill as she looked to her mother with a radiant smile.

Alejandra smiled as Graham walked up. "This your friend, Alice?" he asked.

"No. Well, not yet. This is the woman who is going to wrestle you boys for haircuts. Meet Alejandra." Alice motioned towards the dark-haired woman beside her, and Graham's sharp gaze narrowed at the unexpected guest.

"Graham Hastings." He shook her hand. "And I don't need a haircut." He pointed his annoyed gaze on Alice as she crossed her arms in challenge.

"Tell that to your fiancé, Graham. She's on board to help get you in that chair, whether you like it or not."

"That so?" Graham's defiant tone had Julia breezing from the guest house porch and straight into his arms. She planted a firm kiss on his lips that immediately smoothed his rough edges.

"I just love seeing you ride up on a horse," she whispered, stealing another small kiss before turning her warmth towards Alejandra. "Thank you for coming all the way out here, Alejandra. I'm Julia, the bride-to-be in desperate need of your talents."

The women shook hands. "It's great to be here. Thank you for giving me the opportunity. I brought everything we might need to experiment."

Julia clapped her hands in excitement. "Load me up. I'll help you carry it over. This is where we have you set up for the men's haircuts." Julia pointed to the chair and table on the porch. "Graham, honey, you're first."

He frowned and she laughed. "Don't give me that look. You need one, and I figured by going first you could get back to work as soon as you'd like. Now, here." She handed him one of the bags Alejandra removed from her trunk and he obediently walked it over to the porch of the guest house. "He's not as mean as he seems," Julia whispered to her as Hayes walked back up with an excited Ava swinging his hand in hers. Julia beamed at the little girl. "Hello."

"Are you the princess?"

Julia's brows rose as Alejandra blushed. "She thinks brides are princesses," she explained.

Hayes winked at Julia. "She sure is," he answered for her.

Ava's eyes lit up as they soaked in the beautiful Julia. "And is he your prince?" She looked adoringly up at Hayes.

He shook his head in mock disappointment. "I'm afraid not." He pointed towards Graham standing by the guest house waiting patiently for his haircut. "That man there is her prince. He's my older brother."

Ava boldly walked towards Graham and the rest of the new faces sitting around the porch. Her brown eyes bounced from one face to the next and then back to Graham. She tilted her head all the way back to look up at him and then smiled. "He is, Momma! He *is* a real prince!"

Graham's cheeks flushed at having the adoring little girl's attention and Julia softly giggled. "He doesn't know how to respond to that."

Hayes laughed along with everyone else at Ava's assessment. He turned towards Alejandra and noticed the two bags she hoisted in her hands. "Here, let me get those for you." He took them before she could respond. "She's a sweetheart," he complimented as he nodded towards the guest house. "And we appreciate you comin' by. We don't venture out of Parks much." The woman remained silent as she was greeted by everyone. Ruby hopped in front of her and shook her hand, tugging Lawrence in front of the woman. Lawrence flashed his handsome smile and removed his hat to reveal his unruly hair, Alejandra's weighing gaze already surveying what needed to be done.

"I'm Annie." Annie brushed forward and gave her a warm hug of welcome and motioned towards the chair. "I hope this set up will work. The mirrors in the house are just too high up on the wall."

"This is just fine, thank you."

"Oh honey, thank *you*." Annie waved a hand over the group. "We appreciate you comin' out. Now, if any of them give you trouble, you just let me know."

"We won't with you standin' like a hawk." Clint accepted the swat to his arm as Annie sternly eyed him into humble obedience. He bowed his head to avoid her gaze.

"Graham, get on up here and let this lovely woman trim that hair of yours," Annie ordered.

Ava walked beside him up the steps, Graham pausing momentarily to stare down at her as she followed him.

"I think you have a fan." Seth grinned at the little girl and gave a small wave as Graham, uncomfortable with being princely, hurried his pace to the empty chair and waited while Alejandra began digging out a cape to drape over his shoulders and front.

"I'm sorry." she murmured to him. "Ava, here's your bag. Why don't you go over there and color?" She handed the small girl her backpack and the little girl shook her head, sitting in the free rocking chair nearest Graham. She studied him even closer.

"Where did you meet your princess?" she asked.

"Here," Graham replied, his lack of detail causing everyone around him to roll their eyes as they could tell the little girl was eager to know more.

"Did you give her flowers?"

"I have."

"And a ring?"

"Sure did," Graham responded, handing his hat to his brother, Lawrence, behind him.

"And you're going to live happily ever after?"

"That's the plan."

"Though happily might be in question when it comes to Graham," Clint murmured and received another slap from Annie.

"Ava, honey, that's enough questions. Go on now and color me a picture."

"I'm just talking to the prince, Momma. It's not every day we meet a prince."

Alejandra flushed and Hayes walked up to the railing and rested his arms over the opposite side. "Hey there, friend," he greeted. "I was going to give my horse some carrots. Would you want to help me out?" He glanced up to Alejandra for her permission and she gave a thankful, though a little reluctant, nod.

"Really?" Ava hopped to her feet and smoothed a hand over the front of her little pink dress.

"Yep."

"I'm so cool." Ava looked up at her mother with a charming grin and Alejandra waved her on so she could focus on Graham.

"What's your name again, friend?" Ava asked.

"Hayes."

"Hay? Why would your momma and daddy name you Hay? Like after the stuff horses eat?"

He chuckled. "Hayes, not Hay. Though you can call me whatever you like, butter bean."

She giggled, repeating 'butter bean' under her breath as if it were the funniest thing she'd ever heard, as they walked towards Flash to grab his feed bucket.

"The carrots are in the garden. So we'll go dig a few up," Hayes explained.

"But my dress." Ava looked down. "Will I get dirty?"

"Oh, we'll protect that pretty dress. Don't you worry. I'll do the diggin' and you just tell me which ones you want me to grab."

Liking Hayes's friendly offer, Ava nodded with exuberance as they entered the garden tucked between the two houses.

H

Chapter Two

"*Now, Ms. Alejandra,*" Lawrence began, pulling his cowboy hat off of his head and placing it on his knee. "I like my hair."

Ally smiled as she snapped the cape closed behind his neck and then started to comb her fingers through his thick head of hair. "You have a lot of it."

"Thank the Lord in Heaven."

She chuckled. "Well, let's see what we can do with it."

"I like it somewhat long."

"Just not a rat's nest," Alice taunted.

"She's just bitter because Cal's hair ain't as pretty as mine." Lawrence winked in the window at Ally as she dampened his hair with a spray bottle of water.

Alice huffed and resituated herself in the rocking chair, sipping her sweet tea.

"Oh, ease up, Al. Cal will be back in a bit. I saw Hobbs makin' his way over the road back there when I sat down." Lawrence nodded over his shoulder and Alice's gaze flashed to the horizon to see Calvin's dog, along with Graham and Julia's, trotting towards the main house. "She gets all worked up if Cal's late getting done."

"He was supposed to be here at nine," Alice said. "I mean, Clint even made it on time."

"That's because you said a pretty hairdresser was coming. Clint's not going to miss charming a pretty face."

Ally started brushing through Lawrence's hair and he closed his eyes, opening one to peek over at Ruby. She blew him a quick kiss before settling on the top step next to Seth. Annie walked out of the main house, dressed in an apron, and hands on her hips. "Seth! I need some squash."

Seth hopped to his feet, flopping his hat on his head as he rushed towards the garden. "Yes ma'am. How many?"

"A dozen ought to do it." Annie's eyes looked to the guest house as if needing someone else to boss around.

"Did you need help, Annie?" Julia asked.

"Oh no, sweetie, I've got it. There's still some coffee in here if anyone wants to finish it off."

"That would be me." Graham, finished letting Julia gawk over his new haircut, placed his hat on his head. He paused on the top step. "Thank you for the haircut, Ms. Alejandra. I appreciate it."

"You're welcome." She started snipping at Lawrence's hair and she sensed the brother's tension as dark locks started falling to the porch. "I'm not going to leave you bald," she whispered in assurance and he smiled.

Calvin's truck pulled up the drive and Alice hopped to her feet. "About time."

"Don't be too hard on him, Alice," Julia warned. "He was repairing Clint's truck."

"Then why isn't Clint helping?" Alice barked.

"One, I'm right here, so you two can talk like I'm actually present," Clint butted in. "And two, I was obeying you. You said be here at nine." Knowing he'd caught her in a pickle of whether or not to rant at him any further, Alice ignored him and walked to greet Cal with a frustrated earful. The easygoing brother simply slid his arm around her waist, pulled her to him for a quick kiss, and then walked up the steps to the guest house and removed his hat to meet Ally.

"Sorry, I'm late. Looks like you've had plenty to keep you busy."

"She's been combing through that monstrosity." Clint waved towards Lawrence's head and Cal eased onto a step.

"I'll get you a cold drink," Julia offered, and walked into the house.

"Where's Hayes?" Cal asked.

"Oh, he's gatherin' carrots out of the garden and then helping Alejandra's little one feed his horse." Clint nodded towards Graham's house as Graham exited the front door with a coffee thermos while Hayes and Ava walked out of the garden and towards Flash. Ava stopped directly in Graham's path, her hands on her hips.

"Well, let me see," she ordered with full sass that had Ally groaning and turning around to make sure her daughter wasn't being a nuisance. Hayes's pleased expression at her daughter's attitude had her stifling a lecture. Graham obediently removed his hat and let the little girl survey her mother's work. "Yep. I think that will do. Momma did a good job."

"That she did." Graham eyed the basket of carrots. "Were you going to make my horse fat?"

Ava giggled and Graham's lips twitched as she shook her head. "No, Mr. Hay's horse."

"Ah, I see. Well, good. I can't be ridin' a fat horse."

"You're really tall," Ava observed, as Graham continued on his way to Trisket.

"I've been told that a time or two." He handed his thermos to Hayes while he lifted his foot into the stirrup and pulled himself into the saddle. Ava gasped as if witnessing a magical moment, and Hayes bit back a laugh as Graham accepted his coffee with a quick grab. "You keep them all in line now, alright?"

"I will." Ava nodded as if the job were her most important task.

Graham tapped the brim of his hat before clicking his reins and walking Trisket back towards the east pasture.

"Okay, Flash, I'm here with your breakfast." Ava reached into the bucket and grabbed a carrot. "It has dirt on it."

"He won't mind," Hayes assured her.

"He likes to eat dirt?" Her disgusted expression had Hayes chuckling.

"One of his favorite snacks. Do you not like dirt?"

"No. I like crackers as my snack."

"Crackers? What kind of crackers?"

"The fish ones," she replied.

"Ah, I reckon I recall having those a time or two. Good choice."

Ava grinned as Hayes guided her hand towards Flash's mouth and the horse nibbled the carrot from her grasp. They fed a few carrots, Ava growing more comfortable around Flash as they did so, and she absentmindedly stroked his nose as she enlightened Hayes on all things ponies and unicorns.

"I'm afraid she's going to talk his ears off." Ally glanced at her little girl's reflection in the mirror, the sounds of her chatter drifting towards those on the porch.

Julia sat in the closest rocking chair and smiled. "Hayes won't mind in the least. She's precious."

"Thank you." Ally evened out the last of Lawrence's hair and ran her fingers through it, guiding it into submission. She then backed up a step. "What do you think?"

He looked at his reflection in the window. "Well, I'd say, Ally—" He paused. "Can I call you, Ally?"

She smiled. "That's what I tend to go by mostly any way."

"Ah." He perked up at his correct assessment. "Well, *Ally*, I think you just made me the most handsome out of the bunch."

Julia snickered and Lawrence tossed a thumb her direction. "She tell you I was her first choice?"

Ally's brow arched at that news and Julia shook her head on a laugh. "Lawrence, stop spreading rumors. Besides, we all know Ruby's been your girl for ages."

His gaze turned tender as he watched the love of his life through the reflection on the window talking with his family behind him. "Well, I guess you're right about that. But I was Julia's close second." He looked at Julia and waited until she reluctantly agreed.

"Sure, Lawrence. My close second."

"Ha. I knew it." He clapped his hands before Ally removed his cape and shook his hair onto the porch. "Woo-ee, that's a lot of hair. Don't be too jealous, Cal," he called, as the next brother as Alice's boyfriend walked towards Ally with a warm smile.

"I don't think you'll have to take as long with mine." He removed his hat, his hair, already trimmed short, only needed a small touch up, and

Ally settled him into the wooden chair and began dampening the top of his head with the spray bottle. "I'm Calvin."

"Nice to meet you, Calvin." Ally extended her hand. "Alejandra."

He shook her hand and then settled back comfortably, his eyes floating towards Julia. "Everything good here at the house, Julia?"

"Yes. All things are working, despite Alice's disagreement with the oven the other day."

"I heard about that." He grimaced.

"Seth deep-cleaned the oven while we were at work yesterday, so it is back in operating order." Julia grinned as Cal just shook his head at Alice's blunder. "So, Ally," Julia looked her direction and Ally met her gaze briefly before looking back at Cal's hair. "How do you like Sheffield?"

"It's a nice place."

"Nice place?" Cal asked on a laugh. "Where did you come from that Sheffield would be considered nice?"

Ally blushed. "I just meant that it's not bad."

"Ah. There's the truth then. There's nothing pretty about these west Texas towns."

"Your ranch is pretty."

"A hidden gem," Calvin confirmed. "But Parks is dirtier than a toilet seat."

"Eww." Julia laughed. "Good thing Parks has wonderful people then."

Ally chuckled along with them as she agreed that Sheffield seemed to be home to nice people as well. "Ava loves her daycare and that's one of the most important things I look for when moving to a new place. Though she'll start school next year."

Ava's excited squeal could be heard rounding the corner of the house as Lawrence chased her, making growling sounds, and caught her around the sides and lifted her into the air and swung her in circles. "Got you!"

She giggled as he set her to her feet, and she opened her hand to reveal a brown egg. Hayes walked up carrying a small basket full of eggs. "She's pretty helpful. I'm knockin' out chores left and right." He handed the basket to Julia and offered a friendly smile towards Alejandra. He had the bluest eyes she'd ever seen, and beyond that, they were kind. Kindness seemed to run through his veins and make up the most of him. She didn't even know him, and she could tell just by looking at him that he was as genuine as he seemed.

"Thank you for entertaining her. I understand if you need to work. I brought her some activities she could work on."

"Oh, she's fine. We don't have many little ones come out to the ranch. It's fun to see it through her eyes."

He leaned against the porch railing as Graham's screen door creaked and Annie stepped out onto the porch again. Seth hopped to his feet from the steps next to Ruby. "Whatcha need, Annie?" he called.

"Tomatoes. Four."

"Got it." Seth rushed towards the garden.

"If he'd just go work the rows, she wouldn't have to step out every five minutes," Cal suggested.

"He's enjoying the break this morning." Hayes watched as his younger brother gathered more than just tomatoes on his quick garden blitz, Seth unable to help himself from working an entire row while in there. He hurried the tomatoes into Graham's house.

"Annie must be making a feast." Hayes rubbed a hand over his stomach. "You and Ava should stay for supper, Alejandra. We'd love to have you."

Her hands fumbled slightly, and Cal's eyes glanced up at her fidgeting before she recovered herself. But she sure did like the way Hayes said her name.

"That's a sweet offer, but I imagine I'll be done long before supper."

"We still have to do my makeup," Julia reminded her.

"You're already pretty as a picture, Julia, what could you possibly need?" Hayes asked with apparent confusion.

She patted his hand in thanks. "For my bridal portraits."

"Ah."

"Well, Annie's going to expect you to stay, just so you know." Hayes nodded his attention back towards Ally. "And she'll bring lunch out here in an hour or so, but if she's asking for squash, I can tell you right now, she's already startin' supper too."

"You think she's makin' her fried squash?" Cal asked, the thought making both brothers salivate.

"I hope so."

"Or her squash casserole," Julia added and all three of them hummed in pleased accord.

"You guys are making me hungry," Ally chuckled as they all nodded.

"See? Now you have to stay." Julia took a sip of her sweet tea as Ruby walked up.

"I have to head back to the diner. Kara called. Lunch crowd is already starting to filter in." She looked to Ally. "Thanks for taming Lawrence's hair. It's been driving me nuts."

"No problem."

"If you're still here later this evening, I may have you trim mine too."

"Sure." Ally smiled at the black-haired beauty as she gave Julia a brief hug and squeezed Hayes's hand in passing.

"Lawrence!" Ruby yelled, and Lawrence, flat on his back in the front yard of Graham's house with Ava beside him staring up at cloud shapes, hopped to his feet. "I've got to head out."

Lawrence swept her into a deep dip and planted a solid, but tender kiss on her lips, before nudging her towards her car. "You come back for supper, Ruby Cole," he called after her.

Ruby's flushed face and bright smile carried her on light feet towards her car as she waved to the rest of the crew.

"So much kissing around here these days," Hayes acknowledged.

Alice emerged from within the guest house, carrying a loaded tray of chips and dips. "I like kissing." She wiggled her eyebrows towards Cal and the brother grinned.

"Me too," Julia sighed, thinking of Graham.

"Alright now, I didn't mean to turn you all into mush. Lord knows we have enough of that around here too."

"Jealous." Alice turned her attention to Ally. "You married, Ally? Or seeing someone?"

"Alice," Julia hissed. "That is none of your business."

Alice shrugged unapologetically. "What? It's conversation."

Ally shook her head. "No. I'm not, to both questions."

Alice sent Hayes an encouraging glance that had him rolling his eyes at her thought of matchmaking. "Don't tell Annie," Alice replied. "She'll have you picked out for one of these goons."

"Hey, we're not all bad. I mean, you think I'm alright," Cal defended.

"I've had a lifetime to let you grow on me."

He smirked as Julia rolled her eyes behind her friend's back.

"You're such a romantic, Al," Hayes complimented and received a playful punch from their friend.

Ally dusted Cal's collar and unsnapped the cape. "You're all set."

Cal ran a hand over his hair before placing his hat back on his hat. "Thank you, ma'am." He punched Hayes's shoulder. "Tag. Your turn."

"What about me?" Clint asked. "I've been waiting the longest."

"I'm not done with your truck. Give me a half hour, then it's all yours."

"Ah. Gotcha." Clint settled back against the porch post. "Guess I'll just have to enjoy my Friday with the ladies a bit longer then."

Hayes removed his hat. His hair, though somewhat longer than normal, was still in better shape than Lawrence's was, and Ally felt her fingers tingle at the thought of running her fingers through it. He sat, handing his hat to Julia as he situated himself underneath the cape. Ally dampened his hair and began her work, ordering herself to remain calm as his blue eyes watched her like a hawk. "Your girl's real sweet."

"Thanks. She's... well, a mess. In a good way." Ally grinned as Ava and Lawrence sat on the front of Graham's porch. Annie having brought a tray of snacks, watched them munch a minute before walking back inside to prepare her meal.

"Brave one too," Hayes added. "Not scared of the horses. Usually, little kids take a while to warmup to them, but it was all I could do to keep her from climbing up in the saddle."

"Bravery or stubbornness, I'm not sure which one is more prevalent in Ava these days. She has a whimsical view of horses still. Danger is not in her vocabulary." Ally's hands paused a moment, her fingers slightly fishing around in the top of Hayes's head.

"What is it?" he asked, worry in his eyes. "I don't have a bald spot, do I?"

She giggled a minute before retrieving a clump of dried dirt and grass. "I think this is the first time I've ever trimmed hair and grass at the same time." She handed him the dirt clot as he flushed.

"Oh, I, uh—" He looked to Julia for help, and she patted his knee. "I came straight from the stalls."

"At least it wasn't manure," Clint added. "Hayes is typically covered in it from head to toe."

"I'm a natural fertilizer wherever I go," he agreed. "Part of the job."

"So enchanting." Alice cringed. "What every woman wants is a man that smells like horse dung."

"It's an acquired taste," Hayes defended.

"I like it," Julia interrupted. "Well, not the poop smell, per se, but I like when Graham smells like his work. There's something... masculine about it. I don't know." She wafted her hand in the air as if smelling. "Like Cal, Alice, when he's worked on machinery all day. He smells like oil and grime."

"You saying you like the way my man smells?" Alice asked with a tilt to her lips.

Julia rolled her eyes at the insinuation. "No. I'm saying you do. You've told me more than once. Graham smells like sunshine, dirt, sweat, and cows. Cal smells like oil and grease. Hayes smells like horses." Julia waved her hand towards the attentive brother and he bit back a smile at her attempt of softening the blow of knowing he currently smelled.

"What about me?" Clint asked. "What do I smell like?"

"Like unfinished projects and excuses," Alice combatted.

Everyone laughed as Clint took offense, standing to his feet to leave.

"I was going to say trouble," Julia amended.

Clint turned at that. "Oh, now see, I'll take that one." He flashed a devilish smile as he sat back down.

"Mr. Hay." Ava's voice carried over to them as she climbed the steps to the porch. "Mr. Lawrence said you have some ponies. Ponies fit for a princess like me. Is that true?"

Hayes caught Ally's gaze in the mirror, and she gave a nod that it was okay if he answered truthfully to her daughter. "I sure do."

"Can I ride one?"

Ally paused and looked down at her daughter. "Ava, no ma'am. We are not here to ride horses today. Momma is working. Mr. Hayes has work to do, too, once I'm done."

"I'm just asking, Momma. There's no harm in asking." Ava turned her attention back to Hayes and stood by his knee, watching her mother work on his hair. "Don't trim too much, Momma, or he won't look like Ms. Julia's prince."

Julia chuckled behind her as Ava's brown eyes surveyed her closely. "You know that, Mr. Hay."

"Know what?"

"That you look like Ms. Julia's prince."

"We tend to get that every now and then. Graham's old, though. Like, super old," Hayes added, and flicked a quick wink at Julia.

"He didn't look old to me." Ava crossed her arms. "He's handsome."

"Ava Marie," Ally shushed.

Julia slipped an arm over Ava's shoulders and tugged her into a side hug. "I couldn't agree more, Ava."

"You have a princess, Mr. Hay?"

"I sure don't. Not yet."

"Are you looking for one?" Ava asked.

"Ava—" Ally turned her full attention on her daughter. "That is enough. Now you need to go get your bag and color something. Sit and be quiet now."

"But I don't want to be quiet, Momma. There's too many people to talk to."

"She has a point," Alice pointed out with a sly smile towards Ally.

"Obey, Ava Marie," Ally reiterated and watched as her daughter's shoulders slumped slightly, her feet slowly shuffling to the edge of the porch where her backpack rested amongst Ally's bags of supplies.

She paused directly in front of Hayes. "If you're looking for a princess, Mr. Hay, I've got some ideas." She sensed her mother's disapproval and continued on her way as the Hastings brothers and friends bit back their laughs.

Alice looked to Ally in pure pleasure. "The more I get to know her, the more I like her, Ally.

H

Chapter Three

"*Alejandra, spoon a bit* more on your plate, honey." Annie handed the dish of squash casserole over to Ally and then looked at Seth's plate next to her. "You too, Seth. There's plenty."

I'm already on my second helping, Annie," Seth replied with a rub to his full stomach.

"And I couldn't possibly eat another bite," Ally continued. "It was all so delicious. Thank you for including us." She looked to her daughter across the table, sitting between Julia and Lawrence. Ava chatted as if she'd known them for years.

Hayes watched as Lawrence placed his spoon on his nose and challenged Ava to see who could hold it the longest. She fogged up her spoon with a deep breath and then placed it on her small nose. Julia counted the seconds. Lawrence, though smooth about it, purposely lost, and Ava's triumphant hoot had even Graham grinning. It was nice having a little one around the place. The excitement and joy little Ava had was contagious, and everyone seemed in good spirits after a long day. He also realized he couldn't wait for Julia and Graham to have little ones of their own, so they'd have a young one's presence on the ranch all the time.

"Hayes, honey," Annie interrupted his thoughts. "How's that bronc coming? You give up on it yet?"

"Never." He flashed a quick smile. "He's a good horse. Just needs time."

"You said that two months ago," Clint reminded him.

"And in two months he's come a long way. How would you feel if someone gave up on you after only two months?"

"Then he'd never find a woman," Alice muttered, and the brothers laughed.

"I *choose* to be single," Clint pointed out.

"Riiiiiight," Seth jested. "And how long have you been swooning over Kara?"

Clint's cheeks flushed a bit as he denied the insinuation, but everyone knew he had a sweet spot for the new recruit over at Sloppy's Diner.

"I've got nothing going with Kara, nor do I intend to, because I leave for New Mexico in August. If I'm going to be gone for months, I don't need a woman here." Clint crossed his arms, his eyes staring at an aloof Graham as the oldest brother continued eating his supper and not engaging in an argument over Clint's plans.

"Well, good to know we have until August to put up with you," Lawrence chimed in. "Gives us time to get the spraying in before you go."

"Yeah, what is the status on that, Graham?" Calvin asked. "We still planning on spraying this month?"

"Yes." Graham looked up from his plate and nodded. "I'm meeting with Philip this week to order chemical."

"There's one more brother," Annie explained to Ally. "Philip. He runs the feed store in town. He dates this lovely girl named Helena. You'll just love her."

"I'm sure she's got plenty of names already swimmin' around in her head, Annie," Hayes said. "Don't confuse her further."

"Well, Hayes Matthew," Annie began in her no-nonsense manner, "I am mentioning dear Philip because Helena is to be one of Julia's bridesmaids and will more than likely be getting her face done by Alejandra for the wedding as well."

"Ah." Hayes blushed at the scolding and gave a small tilt of his head in apology towards Ally for butting into their conversation.

"Julia, when is the day for bridals?" Annie asked. "I want to make sure I'm here for it."

"Two weeks," Julia replied, sliding her hand towards Graham's on the table and giving it an excited squeeze.

"I don't have to be there, do I?" Graham asked, still scarred from having engagement photos taken a few weeks prior.

Julia laughed. "No. In fact, you can't be there because I will be in my wedding dress. And you, sir, are not allowed to see it before the big day."

"But I get to." Lawrence winked at his older brother.

"And me." Hayes nodded enthusiastically, liking that Graham seemed to grow even more displeased as each of his brothers taunted their privilege in front of him.

"And all of you better be polished up," Alice ordered. "Because Jewels wants pictures with all of you."

"Of us?" Hayes asked. "Why?"

Julia looked down the table at him. "Because I want a picture with all of my future brothers. That is, if you guys don't mind."

"Mind?" Seth held a hand to his heart. "We'd all be honored, Jewels."

Her smile softened towards the youngest brother as his face slowly paled. "What am I supposed to wear?"

"Don't worry, jeans are fine," Julia assured him with a light trickle of laughter.

"Dress like you're going to church." Annie patted Seth's hand.

"You'll have to remind me when the time comes." Lawrence placed his napkin beside his plate. "I'm likely to forget what day it is, and I'll show up all nasty."

"That's fine too," Julia assured him.

"We'll most likely be in the middle of sprayin'," Graham stated.

"And sprayin' can wait a few hours while we sweep your woman off her feet," Cal replied with a smirk. "Count me in, Julia."

"Does this mean we have to get our hair cut again before then?" Seth asked, brushing a hand over his freshly trimmed hair. "I mean, in a couple weeks I might need another trim to look spiffy enough."

Laughing, Julia shook her head. "Ally will be here, though, if you think you need a good trim. She's going to do my hair and makeup for the photos."

"And me!" Ava raised her hand in excitement. "Right, Momma? I can come too?"

"We'll see. You may have daycare that day."

Ava crossed her arms in dissatisfaction. "That's not fair. I want to come too."

"You're more than welcome to come, Ava," Julia invited. "If your mom wants to bring you."

Ava perked in her seat. "Maybe I can ride around with you, Mr. Gwaham, since you can't see your princess."

Everyone waited for Graham's response.

"It'd be my pleasure, Ava."

"See, Momma, I'm more than welcome."

Hayes laughed at the girl's enthusiasm as Ally caught his amused gaze with one of her own.

"We'll see," she reiterated.

"Now listen here, butter bean," Hayes leaned forward as Ava giggled at the nickname. "If you're off riding with Graham, who's going to help me with the horses?"

Her eyes lit from within at the thought and she looked to Graham and then to Hayes. "This is hard," she said, her comment bringing a smile to Graham's face as he chuckled next to Julia.

"How about you help Hayes there with the horses and after the pictures, you and your Momma can go on a ride to see the ranch?" Graham offered.

"We'd love that, Mr. Gwaham. Won't we, Momma?"

Ally nodded her thanks as Annie stood to gather empty plates. She followed suit and Annie waved her back down into the chair and then pointed to the only brother paying any attention, Hayes. He stood and began gathering the plates and followed Annie to the kitchen to help with washing.

"You best keep a close eye on that little sweetheart if she's in the stalls, Hayes," Annie whispered. "A whimsical heart typically blocks out any concern for danger."

"I will. There's rules to follow when in there, and I'll make sure to make them known."

Annie patted his back before heading back to the table and leaving him to wash.

∞

Ally lightly feathered and fluffed the dark hair of Ms. Joanna Mason as she watched the features of the pretty woman in her chair light up with pleasure. "How's that?"

"It's perfect. Absolutely perfect." Joanna held up the picture of the magazine cutout she'd brought with her. "I think it's even better than the photo."

The bell on the salon door jingled and a hush fell over the crowded salon as a tall man with a neatly trimmed beard, dark hair, and kind eyes stepped into the building. He removed his cowboy hat and gave a friendly nod and smile towards Sandy.

"May I help you?" she asked.

"Yes ma'am. I was hoping to speak with Alejandra Garcia."

Everyone's gaze swung from the man to Ally, Joanna tampering down an excited "Oh my," as she watched the handsome stranger walk towards Ally, hat in hand.

"You're Ally?" he asked.

"I am."

"Philip Hastings." He extended a hand and she relaxed, realizing it was the last remaining brother of the large brood over in Parks. "I'm sorry to barge in like this, but my brothers mentioned you were the woman to go to for a haircut, and well, I found myself in Sheffield today and thought I'd see if you could fit me in."

"If she won't, I will!" Dolores, a short stubby woman of about fifty years old called from her salon chair as she smacked her gum and flicked a quick wink at Philip.

"I don't mind at all," Ally said. "I'm almost done here and can be with you in just a minute."

"Thank you." Philp walked over to a vacant chair in between two elderly women awaiting their turns for a new style. They eyed him with pure interest as he sat with his cowboy hat resting on his knee.

"My, my, my…" Joanna whispered. "If only I were in your shoes today."

Ally pretended not to hear as she shook out the cloak and helped Joanna out of the chair. "I've heard of the Hastings brothers, but never have I had the luxury of seeing one in person. Are they all as impressive as that one?"

Ally, cornered for a response, just simply nodded as she walked Joanna towards the cash register and began walking her through the checkout process. The door swung open with a quick swish, the bell jingling wildly as Hayes Hastings walked inside with wild eyes and a hurried step. His eyes landed on Ally first and then his brother. "I thought you said it would be like five minutes?" he asked Philip.

"I'm next." Philip nodded in Ally's direction and Hayes took a calming breath as he tipped his hat towards her. "Ally, good to see ya. Ladies." He nodded to the other women in the room. "I can't keep him calm much longer." Hayes motioned over his shoulder towards the truck and trailer parked across the street, an antsy bronc nervously side-stepping inside the trailer. "The traffic scares him."

"Then move the truck." Philip fished his keys out of his pocket and handed them to his brother.

"Thanks. I'll be back." Hayes darted out the door and across the street, every head in the salon leaning to gaze out the window at his retreating form.

Joanna Mason walked towards the door, reluctant to leave now that some fresh excitement and handsome faces had arrived. She flashed Ally a grateful smile. "I'll be seeing you, Ally. Thanks for the cut." She fished in her purse for her keys as Hayes walked back towards the salon. He opened the door and held it wider for her to exit. "Well, thank you." She flashed her most alluring smile and Hayes, completely unaware of the flirtation, tipped his hat and stepped inside, ignoring Joanna's lingering on the sidewalk.

"Philip." Ally waved him back towards her booth, Hayes hot on his brother's heels. Philip sat in the black chair and Hayes took a seat in one of the free hair-dryer chairs.

He grinned at Ally. "How's your day going, Ally?"

Still a bit out of sorts at the unexpected visit and stares from around the room, Ally forced a smile. "Good."

"Sorry to just show up on you like this," Philip apologized again. "But when I'm in town, I try to knock out as much as possible. I don't venture out of Parks much unless it's to go to Midland."

"And I hardly ever venture out of the ranch unless it's to pick up a new horse or to eat at Sloppy's," Hayes picked up the conversation. "You're the lucky lady that has to deal with both of us today, though we'll be buggin' Julia and Alice at the vet clinic here shortly."

"It's not a problem at all. I had some openings today, so it's easy to fit you in." Ally snapped the cape around Philip's neck. "And nice to meet you, Philip. I heard a bit about you the other day at the ranch."

"Please do not let anything my brothers said about me taint your first impression of me."

She chuckled. "They only said good things."

"Of course, we did." Hayes flipped through a women's hair magazine as he danced his eyes up to meet his brother's. "We spoke mostly about how Helena is too good for you."

Philip smirked. "Can't argue that point."

Ally grinned at their banter as her cell phone dinged with a text message. "I apologize. I need to make sure it's not the daycare."

"No problem." Philip waved her concern away as she swiped her finger over the screen and her face fell. Irritation, frustration, annoyance, and a touch of sympathy ate at her heart as she read the message from Ava's teacher. Ava was having a difficult day: not listening, being rude to the other kids, and begging to go home. It'd become her routine as of late, and Ally was at wits' end trying to figure out why her daughter was suddenly acting out. Ally's mother insisted it was due to the lack of a male presence in her life to help with discipline. Ally, however, chalked it up to discontentment. Her daughter had been attending the daycare and had yet to truly connect with any of the other kids. She never mentioned friends. She begged every morning not to go. And if Ally had an alternative, she'd have Ava somewhere else in a heartbeat.

"Everything okay?" Hayes' voice had her glancing up.

"Oh, um, yes. Sort of."

"Ava okay?" he asked.

"She's fine… just… being a nuisance, apparently."

Ally typed a quick response to the teacher and then set her phone back on the work counter.

"Atta girl." Hayes grinned. "I'd think she'd be a little pistol in class."

"She is." Ally snipped at Philip's hair. "That's the problem."

"People don't know how to handle spirited kids these days." Hayes shook his head in disappointment.

"And you do?" Philip laughed at the absurdity.

"Well, no, but I know what a spirited horse is like and putting its nose in the corner never works. I imagine kids are somewhat the same." He held up his hands in surrender to Ally's motherhood. "But I'm not a parent, so what do I know."

"Exactly," Philip added. "And you never had a rebellious bone in your body."

"I did too. Once."

"Oh really? When?"

"When I wanted to start the horse training and go against Graham. I pushed on that for years before he finally cracked."

"That's not rebellion, that's stubbornness."

"Doesn't that kind of go hand in hand?" Hayes asked. "Besides, you're the rebel of the family."

"I'd hardly call myself a rebel." Philip's eyes humored as he caught Ally's gaze in the mirror. "I don't work on the ranch, therefore I am the family black sheep who bucked the system. And I'd hardly say two grown men choosing their life's work compares to a small girl in daycare."

"You're more than welcome to bring her out to the ranch anytime, Ally," Hayes invited. "She seemed to enjoy it out there. Give her a place to run a bit wild and free."

"The last thing Ava needs is to be wilder," Ally chuckled. "But thank you."

Her phone dinged again as she finished brushing off the hair snips from Philip's neck and unsnapping his cape. She glanced at the message and sighed. "Perfect timing, I guess. You're my last one for the day." She smiled at Philip. "And I have to go get Ava."

Hayes glanced at the clock. "It's only three."

"Yes, well, she's worn out her daily welcome." Ally's voice sounded tired and frustrated as she grabbed the broom from behind her booth and began sweeping Philip's hair. The brother eyed his cut in the mirror before fishing in his pocket for his wallet.

Hayes motioned towards outside. "Come to the clinic."

"I'm sorry?" Ally asked.

"Come to the vet clinic after you pick up Ava."

"Why?" Ally asked.

"Because I think I know exactly what you both need for today."

Philip's brow rose at his brother's adamancy and watched as the beautiful woman's tan skin flushed a moment.

Hayes stood, twisting his hat in his hand. "Come on, Ally, give me a chance."

She studied him a moment, his bright blue eyes shining with sincerity. She noticed not a sound could be heard in the salon as the other women waited on bated breath to hear her reply. "Alright. I'll swing by."

"Good deal. We'll wait until you get there."

He patted Philip's shoulder as he walked towards the door, his brother following after him. He handed several bills to Ally, and she fumbled. "This is too much. Let me get you some change."

"Keep the change," Philip told her. "You fit me in and tolerated my brother. You've earned it."

Thankful, Ally nodded.

"See you in a bit." Philip placed his hat back on his head and gave it a small tap before following Hayes out towards the truck.

H

Chapter Four

Hayes waited on the steps of the veterinary clinic as Alice surveyed his newest purchase. She ducked when the horse swung its neck around and over her head before she could sneak out of its way. "He's got some trauma," she reported. "Looks like he's got a few messed up ribs, but it's hard for me to tell because he won't let me touch him."

"I figured he did." Hayes pointed towards a protrusion on the horse's side. "That one of them?"

"Yep. I could sedate him and adjust it, but not here. It'd be better to do it at the stables where he's more comfortable."

"Can you do it this evening?" Hayes asked.

Alice heaved a sigh and rolled her eyes. "You boys. Just because I date your brother now, you think I'm available at your every whim."

Hayes waited patiently.

"Yes, I can do it this evening. Have him ready by the time I get home."

"Good deal."

Ally's car pulled into the parking lot and Alice's brows rose in surprise as Hayes straightened to his full height. "Interesting..." Alice murmured, catching the nervous gaze of Hayes as he watched Ally and Ava step out of the small car.

Philip leaned patiently against the trailer and motioned towards the two. "He invited them here."

"What for?" Alice asked.

"The kid needs a clinic fix," Hayes said.

"The clinic is not a daycare, Hayes," Alice muttered.

"It won't be. They won't be in the way, I promise. I already spoke to Julia."

Alice smiled at an approaching Alejandra. "Got yourself a varmint problem?" Alice swooped a hand over Ava's ponytail and gave it a playful tug as Ally placed a hand on her daughter's shoulder.

"Mr. Hay?" Ava's face split into a beaming smile as she lunged at his legs. "I thought I'd never see you again!"

He laughed. "Oh, now butter bean, I thought we were friends."

She nodded emphatically and looked up at Philip. "Who are you?"

"Ava—" Ally warned. "Be polite. This is another Hastings. This is Mr. Philip."

"Another one?" Ava's eyes rounded. "Why are you all so tall?"

Philip chuckled as he extended a hand to the little girl. "Because we like the weather better up here."

Ava's eyes flashed to the horse behind Hayes. "You have to take him to Ms. Alice so she can doctor him?"

"Yep." Hayes pointed to his friend and complimented. "She's the best around."

"What's wrong with him?"

"Well," Hayes motioned for her to step a few feet away from the trailer and he pointed to the horse's side. "he's hurt pretty bad. The people that owned him before me weren't that nice to him."

"So you rescued him?"

"I sure did."

"Like a prince rescues a princess?"

"Something like that, I guess."

"Is he nice?"

"Not really," Alice supplied. "But I wouldn't be either if I was hurt as bad as he is."

"Can you help him?" Ava asked.

"Yep. Going to tonight when we get home," Alice reported.

"Good." Ava gave a firm nod that had Alice biting back a smile at the girl's authoritative manner.

A silence lingered a moment before Hayes rallied and clapped his hands. "Now, I asked your momma to bring you to the clinic today for a very special reason."

"Really? What for?" Ava asked, her eyes full of wonder and admiration as she looked from Hayes and then to Ally.

"Well, Ms. Julia said there's a task she needs help with that only the smartest of little girls can help with."

"I'm smart!" Ava bounced on her feet and shook her mother's hand. "Tell him, Momma. I'm smart!"

"You're very smart." Ally smiled down at her daughter.

"Are you?" Hayes looked pleased. "I was hoping you would say that, because I told Ms. Julia I knew the perfect little girl for the job. Come on, I'll show ya." He waved for them to follow, Alice and Philip lingering behind to survey the horse some more.

Hayes walked into the clinic and offered a friendly wave towards Julia behind the counter, her scrubs covered in cartoon dogs and bones. She knelt in front of Ava and gave the girl a warm hug. "I'm so glad you came." She stood and rubbed a welcoming hand on Ally's back.

"Your smartest little girl is reporting for duty," Hayes told Julia.

"Oh, wonderful." Julia's eyes warmed. "Will you help me, Ava?"

"Sure. But with what? Mr. Hay hasn't said."

"A very special job." Julia waved them towards a back room and opened the door. In Alice's office, nudged to the side, was a large crate with a golden Labrador and ten fluffy yellow balls of fur. Ava squealed in delight at the sight of the puppies and looked up at Julia expectantly. "They have to be played with and I just haven't had the time today. Do you think you could show each of them a little attention for me?"

Ava looked up at Ally, her dark little eyes begging. Ally nodded.

Ava slid to her knees, her hands already diving into the fluff and receiving welcoming licks from the fumbling puppies as they climbed over one another to reach her. She giggled and looked up at Hayes. "Thanks, Mr. Hay."

He gave a firm nod as he looked at Julia and Ally. "I better head back to the ranch if I'm going to get that horse settled in a stall before Alice comes home."

Julia gently rubbed a hand on his arm. "I'll be cooking chicken caponata tonight at Graham's if you get hungry for supper."

"I don't even know what that is, but you can count me in. Maybe. If the horse settles in okay."

"Sleeping in a stall is fine, Hayes, but not on an empty stomach."

He blushed as he tapped his hat. "Yes ma'am. I'll be seeing you." He started to walk to the door and Ally reached out and grabbed his arm. Her touch sent a current shooting up his skin and his eyes sparked when they found hers.

She quickly removed her hand, as if burned, and inhaled a deep breath. "Thank you, Hayes, for... this." She waved her hand at her daughter who was now laying on the floor and giggling as puppies crawled on top of her, some licking her face and ears. "It was much needed."

"Loving and tending to animals is one of the best ways to end a difficult day. I'm glad it's something she enjoys. Take care, Ally." He ducked his way out and Julia watched as Ally's gaze and body leaned towards the window of the office and the woman's dark gaze watched Hayes up until the point he and Philip drove away.

"Well," Julia eased onto her knees, breaking the trance that held Ally's gaze out the window. "let's say we give them some names and each one gets a different colored collar."

Ava sat up, swiping her hair from her eyes. She lifted the runt of the litter, the small puppy snuggling into her embrace. "This one needs a blue collar," she said, "And I'm going to name him Hay."

J   ulia looked up at Ally as the woman found her way to her knees by her daughter and gently stroked a hand over the puppy's fur. "I guess a little hero worship is normal these days," she murmured, making Julia chuckle.

"I think Hay is a great name, Ava. He's kind of the same color as hay too."

"Not hay, Ms. Julia. Hay. Like Mr. Hay. He's my friend."

"Ah. I see. Well, it's a great name, nonetheless. How about this one?" She lifted another puppy and Ava gleefully named the next one while Julia slipped a pale pink collar around its neck.

∞

She'd tucked Ava into bed. She'd read the customary two books. She'd listened to her daily recap. And she'd turned on the unicorn nightlight and cracked the bedroom door before leaving Ava to her sweet dreams about golden puppies. Now, Ally poured herself a glass of wine, walked to the old, worn out chair that had come from her grandparent's house in Mexico, and tucked her feet underneath her. She reached for the book on the lamp table and settled into what she hoped was a few hours of uninterrupted reading. Ava hadn't slept through the night since moving to Sheffield two years ago. Ally had yet to understand why, other than her little girl hadn't adjusted to their new life here.

Ava despised attending daycare. But they didn't live with Ally's parents anymore and her mother wasn't nearby to watch Ava when Ally went to work. The move was supposed to be good for both of them. A fresh start. It was time for Ally to find her own feet again. A bad relationship shouldn't hold a person down for half a decade. Only it had. She'd shied away from friends, fun, and any sort of relationship that required knowing someone beyond a first name basis. She could blame her ex, Derrik, but it wasn't only his fault. Had he been horrible to her and to Ava? Yes. But Ally stayed. She tried to convince herself it was the best decision. That Ava needed her dad in her life. But when the father of your child doesn't want that responsibility, it's time to leave, not linger for three more years and hope his mind changed. But that's what Ally did. Until finally, her own mother and father showed up and intervened. They'd taken the last of the crying phone calls from her that they could handle, and within a day, she and Ava were tucked comfortably away in the house Ally'd grown up in, showered with love from her parents. Now, she spent most nights reading the hours away, instead of chatting with her mom into the wee hours of the morning. She and Ava didn't own a television, as Ally couldn't quite justify the expense of one yet. The cost of daycare and house rent required most of her income until she built a steady clientele at the salon. And that had been a struggle too. Though since joining Sandy's Salon, things were looking up. And she'd just booked Julia McComas and her bridal portraits. Ally planned to do a stellar job, so she'd get the coveted wedding booking as well. And the Hastings family had drastically overpaid her for their haircuts at the ranch last week. She'd tried to give some of the money back to Julia, but the woman insisted it was more for her tolerance of the rambunctious brood than for the haircuts themselves.

She liked the Hastings family. They were warm and kind. She liked Annie too, though she hadn't quite figured out how she fit into the picture yet. And what Hayes had done for Ava today by setting up the time with the puppies touched a part of Ally's heart that'd been dormant for the last three years. What surprised her more was that he'd done it without asking for anything in return. He saw a need and just simply helped, as though that's what he did every day. Perhaps he did. She didn't know him well enough to know that yet. But he was compassionate. She saw that in his offer to her and Ava, as well as his care for the wounded horse he'd just rescued. Compassionate men were a rare species. Other than her own father, she hadn't come across many in her lifetime. Her phone dinged and she glanced at the text message shining on her screen.

Julia McComas: *"Sorry to message so late, but Ava left her bracelet at the clinic today. Would love to get this back to her."*

Ally: *"Sorry about that."*

Julia: *"No worries. Do you have plans this weekend?"*

Ally: *"Only a couple of cuts on Saturday morning."*

Julia: *"You and Ava come out to the ranch Saturday afternoon. We can do lunch and I can give Ava her bracelet back."*

Ally: *"I can just swing by the clinic tomorrow after work, if that's easier."*

Julia: *"Easier, but not as much fun."* She'd added a winking smile face to the end of her text.

Ally: *"Alright. Saturday afternoon it is."*

Julia: *"Yay! See you then."*

Ally set her phone aside and felt the odd sensation of joy rise up in her chest at the thought of possibly having a new friend. She'd tamper that down, though. Best to be realistic. Julia was just being nice. She was a client, nothing more. *But what if?* Ally thought. What if she was able to see Hayes while at the ranch also. Ava would like to see the wounded horse again... to check on it. Who was she fooling? She wanted to see Hayes again, herself. And that thought terrified her.

She shoved Hayes out of her mind and went back to her book until she realized the image in her mind of the main male character had suddenly shifted into Hayes. Hayes talking. Hayes solving a mystery. Hayes's blue eyes sparked with intrigue instead of the brown eyed man described in chapter one. She closed her book with a bit more force than necessary and set it aside. She glanced at her phone and dialed her mother's number. What she needed was the voice that had soothed her over the years. The one woman who could knock some sense into her, figuratively and literally at times if needed.

"Hola, Mamá."

"Mija. Es tarde. ¿Lo que está mal?"

"Nothing is wrong." Ally smiled to herself as she resituated in her chair and took a sip of her wine. "I was just calling to see how your day went."

"Ah." Her mother paused a moment, more than likely debating on whether or not she wanted to press her daughter further for the reason behind her late-night call. Instead, her voice began regaling Ally about her newly planted pots around the porch of their house and the annoying mosquitos that tortured her while completing the task. As was typical with her mom, Ally soon felt better and found herself laughing, ending the call with a light heart and eyes ready for sleep.

H

Chapter Five

He ran his hand over the bronc's silky coat, his fingers lightly trailing over the place where the horse's ribs had been adjusted by Alice. The horse didn't flinch, but instead, continued chomping away on the fresh bucket of oats Hayes provided by way of distraction. Content with the healing process, Hayes stepped out of the stall and walked towards the noisy stall at the end of the barn. This was his ornery charge he'd been determined to break; the horse that allowed a saddle to be placed on his back, but still refused to have a rider, even one as gentle as Hayes. It was true that he'd spent more time on this horse than most he'd broken in the past, but for some reason he connected with this guy. Maybe it was the unbridled and superior attitude the horse possessed, the confidence in knowing he was a beautiful beast full of unrestrained power. Hayes marveled at such creatures, and this bronc was no different. He recognized when he had a fan. And Hayes was definitely a fan. It amazed Hayes how such beautiful creatures were designed with not only animal instincts but individual personalities as well. His beloved Flash had been his horse for close to a decade. Flash was docile, dependable, and loved carrots. He'd nuzzle your pocket for a sugar cube and then ferociously cut cattle from pasture to pasture if need be. He was sharp, trained, and majestic in movement. But this one, mused Hayes as he leaned against the closed gate of the stall, was a force. A force for good or bad, he wasn't sure yet, but a force, nonetheless. A beautiful combination of fury, power, and stubbornness. The horse's ears twitched as the sound of a vehicle door came from outside the barn. More than likely one of his brothers. The horse stepped closer towards him and he extended his hand to see if the bronc would allow him to touch his nose or not.

"Mr. Hay!" A loud little voice startled the horse, and it lunged towards the stall's barricaded door and had Hayes taking a quick step back to avoid the rattle of the door on its hinges.

"Ava!" Alejandra grabbed her daughter's hand and pulled her back behind her, apology written all over her face as Ava, afraid she was in trouble with Hayes, peeked from behind her legs. "I'm so sorry." Ally held a hand to her face. "I'd thought my warnings of entering quietly were taken seriously.

Apparently, I was wrong. I am sorry to intrude like this."

"Not a problem." Hayes offered a warm smile, though his curiosity was piqued as he saw her eyes dart nervously around the barn. "What brings you to my stables?" He glanced at his watch and realized it was well past six and time to call it a day.

"I wanted to thank you." Ally held a shopping bag in her free hand and extended it towards him. "For yesterday at the clinic."

As Hayes stepped closer, Ally took a cautious step back towards the sunlight, as though his presence made her nervous. He smiled in greeting at Ava. "Hey there, Ava. How are you?"

She grinned as she bravely stepped from behind her mother. "I'm good, Mr. Hay. We came to give you supper. Momma makes really good food."

"Supper?" His brows rose as he eyed the bag in Ally's hand. "Is that what that is?" He nodded towards the bag and Ava nodded. "Well, I love supper. I especially love it if two pretty girls bring it to me."

Ava giggled and looked up to find Ally smiling down at her. "Mr. Lawrence told us how to find you," she reported. "He said you were probably reading your horses bedtime stories."

Hayes laughed. "He would think that most likely. I may baby them, but I don't read them books," he commented, more towards Ally than to Ava. "I sure hope you ladies didn't come all this way just to bring me a treat."

"We did," Ava answered, looking up at her mother. "Momma said it was now or never."

Hayes smirked at that and motioned towards outside the barn. He followed behind them, closing the barn doors and then grabbing his cowboy hat off a hook on the outside wall. He tapped it on his leg a couple of times to shake the dust off before plopping it back on his head. "Next time you'll have to get here a little earlier and you can help me feed the horses."

"Really?" Ava asked, her eyes sparkling.

"Sure." Hayes rested his hands on his hips, unsure what to say or do next. Ally still held onto the bag she'd prepared for him and her eyes wandered over the barn and pens. They fluttered back towards him and she flushed.

"Here." She extended the bag, and he graciously took it, bending his head inside to smell the contents. He wasn't sure what it was, but it sent his senses into overdrive. "I hope you like carne asada."

"Like it?" Hayes brows perked. "I absolutely love Mexican food. Thanks. Again, I don't know what I did to deserve this, but I will proudly accept it because now that I've caught a whiff, I don't think I can return it."

"Ava, honey, why don't you head on back to the car, please."

"But Momma—"

"Now, please. I'll be over there in a minute."

Ava's bottom lip pouted a moment before Hayes lightly tapped her nose with his finger. "Thanks for supper, butter bean."

Her frown lifted into a friendly smile. "You're welcome." She skipped towards the car.

"Her teacher said her attitude was a complete turnaround today. Something about the clinic yesterday helped her, and I just can't thank you enough for giving her that opportunity."

Touched that such a small gesture meant so much to her, he nodded. "Animals have a way of healing us. Whether it be anger, fear, frustration, hurt... they just seem to know exactly what we're feeling and then love on us in the way we need. I'm glad the puppies helped smooth out her rough edges, whatever may have caused them. That, and she seems to have an attentive Momma seeing to her needs as well. I think both of those things help."

Ally ran a nervous hand through her hair. "Thanks for saying that. It's been tough lately. Life has been... well, not as I'd hoped, and Ava deserves the best. I'm trying to give that to her, but some days she doesn't see it that way."

"Do kids ever really see what their parents do for them? I mean, they may see a little, but typically most kids are pretty self-centered, myself included when I was younger. We sometimes can't see past our own problems or hurts and even consider how hard our folks are working to make us happy and keep us healthy."

"That's true, I guess," she admitted. "Anyways, I don't want to keep you from heading home, and I definitely didn't come here to air out my problems." She waved her hand as if shooing away their recent conversation, as if he'd think less of her for actually having problems. He definitely didn't think less of her.

"You know, Ava is about the right age to start riding lessons," Hayes suggested.

Ally paused, her steps faltering over a rough patch of ground, Hayes's hand quickly came to her elbow to stabilize her. She bolted from his touch, withdrawing his hold immediately. He briefly held his hand up in a calming motion before dropping it to his side. She sighed in frustration. "Sorry," she fumbled. "Um, I'll think about it."

"A girl who loves horses... might be fun for her."

"And do you teach lessons?" Ally asked.

"A few," Hayes answered, though it had been a couple of years since he had. "Let me know. I certainly don't mind. And since you'll be out here for the portraits and such, I'm assuming we'll be seeing more of you."

"That's only one day," Ally chuckled.

He shrugged. "I don't know much about weddings and all the preparation. I thought it was a consistent thing."

"What? You think a bride will be taking pictures every weekend?"

He rubbed a palm over his stubbled face and his cheeks deepened in color. "I really have no idea. I just assumed you ladies would be tryin' all kinds of different looks or somethin'."

"No." Ally bit back a laugh but a small snicker slipped through and she watched as he kicked a small rock with his boot and avoided her gaze until his embarrassment passed. "Julia found a look she likes and now I just wait until picture day."

"Oh." Disappointment laced his tone, but he tried to hide it by giving a small wave towards Ava in the car. "Again, I don't know much about it all. But my offer still stands. If Ava would like riding lessons, let me know. Or if you would too. I mean, if you like horses," he continued. "You're more than welcome to ride my horses too. Well, a horse, I mean. If you want. Anytime." His words trailed off as his nerves got the best of him, and he cleared his throat and reached for the handle on her car door, eager to end his social agony.

Graham's truck started driving by and paused, turning at the last minute towards the barn upon seeing his brother. He stepped out and walked towards them. "Gotta go to Philip's and order chemical. Want to ride with and get a bite at Sloppy's?"

"Julia not home yet?"

"No. She's making a grocery and errand run before heading back. She'll be in late." He tipped his hat towards Ally. "Ms. Alejandra."

A tap sounded on the window as Ava knocked her fist to get Graham's attention. To Hayes' surprise, his brother's face split into a warm smile as he reached for the handle on the passenger back door. "Well, well, well, who do we have here?"

"Hi, Mr. Gwaham!" Ava gave him an enthusiastic high five as he held up his hand.

"I'll ride with you," Hayes said, bummed he wouldn't be able to dig into the fresh meal in his hands just yet. "I may eat this on the way, and you can get your own order from Sloppy's."

Graham surveyed the bag in his brother's hands and his right brow slightly quirked as his gaze took in Hayes's flushed cheeks and Ally's avoidance of eye contact. "I didn't realize you already had supper plans. I can grab Clint."

"No, no, I'll go. Lord knows Clint doesn't need to be involved with ordering the chemicals for sprayin'."

"We will get out of your hair." Ally reached into the backseat and quickly buckled Ava's car seat.

"Why don't you follow us into town, Ally?" Hayes invited. "It won't take but a minute at Phil's feed store. We could all grab a bite to eat at Slop's."

"Oh, I wouldn't want t—"

"You won't be intruding," Graham interrupted her. "Helena is in town and I'm sure she and Philip will join us as well."

"Can we, Momma? Please? I wanna eat with Mr. Gwaham and Mr. Hay."

"We have supper waiting on us at home," Ally reminded her daughter.

Hayes held up his bag. "It'll keep just fine, won't it? I plan to eat this first thing in the morning."

"Morning?" Ava giggled. "That's not breakfast!" She laughed as he crossed his eyes at her.

"I'll have Julia swing by Slop's on her way home." Graham was already pulling out his cell phone and sending a message to his fiancé.

Ally's hesitancy had Hayes stepping towards her. "No pressure," he whispered, nodding towards his brother's back as Graham stepped towards his truck to focus on his phone. "But we'd love to have you two ladies join us if you can." He held her gaze a moment before she slowly nodded and his face split into a charming smile. "Great. I appreciate this." He held up the bag again. "I'm sorry you went to so much trouble to bring it to me and here we are makin' you turn around and eat in town."

"It was no trouble. And as long as it gets eaten, I'm not picky on when it's consumed."

"Well, I can guarantee it will. It smells amazing."

"Alright," Graham's voice carried over to them. "I hope you don't mind, but I think most of the crew is actually going to meet us over at Sloppy's now."

"That should be a handful. Did anyone think to give Ruby a heads up?" Hayes asked.

"I sent her a text."

"Anyone else riding with us?"

"No. Clint's washin' up, Cal's still underneath his work truck covered in oil, and Seth is ridin' with Lawrence."

Hayes looked at his dirty clothes and his impatient older brother. Though he'd like to clean up himself, he could already tell Graham was eager to get on with his last chore of the day. "I guess I'll see you in a few." He held open Ally's door and she eased into her car. "If you get there before any of us, Ruby will show you where we normally sit."

Her nervous nod told him he and Graham better make their stop at Philip's quick or Ally may chicken out and head back to Sheffield. To prevent that he added, "Or you can just follow us to the feed store. We won't take but a few minutes."

Her shoulders relaxed at this suggestion and he closed her door, jogging towards Graham's truck. He set the bag of food at his feet and buckled his seat belt. He glanced up when he realized Graham sat staring at him. "What?"

"She's bringing you food now?"

"It's a thank you gift."

Graham bit back a grin at his brother's unease and turned the wheel towards town.

∞

"How much do you need?" Philip asked, looking to Calvin as they both studied the order slip on Philip's counter. Their heads popped up in unison as Graham, Hayes, Ally, and Ava walked inside.

"What are you doing here? I thought you were still working on your truck?" Graham asked Calvin.

"Finished up, so I thought I'd come order the chemical we need for sprayin'."

"You?" Graham challenged. "I said I was going to do it."

"Figured while I was here, I'd take care of it." Cal shrugged his shoulders as if it were no big deal.

"Do you even know how to get a 1% mix?"

"If by 1% you mean 1% of a 30-gallon tank, then yeah." Cal straightened for the duel that was about to ensue. "It's 128 ounces. And if you're wanting 30 gallons of chemical then that would be 128 ounces multiplied by 30, which would then give you 3,840 ounces. Then you divide that by 100 and you get 38 ounces. Is that right, Phil?" Cal asked, crossing his arms over his chest, as Philip checked his numbers on the calculator.

"That looks right to me."

Hayes shot Ally an apologetic look as his brothers continued to square off.

"And what makes up that 30 gallon tank?" Graham continued.

Cal groaned. "38 ounces of picloram, 38 ounces of Fluroxpyr, and 10 ounces surfactant to every 30-gallon tank."

"Alright, good." Graham stuffed his hands in his pockets. "Now what about for mesquite?"

"Graham!" Hayes waved a hand in between the brothers. "Cal obviously knows what he's doing. Philip does too. Why don't you just let them get the order done, look over it, and then let's all go eat?"

Forgetting Ally and Ava stood to the side patiently waiting, Graham harumphed and stepped towards the counter to finish the order Cal had started.

Calvin retreated towards Hayes, mumbling about 'ungrateful older brothers' and halted his mutterings to greet Ally and Ava warmly. "You two ladies joining us for supper over at Sloppy's?"

"Sure am." Ava beamed. "Mr. Hay invited us."

"Did he?" Cal winked at his younger brother before looking down at Ava. "I'm glad he did. Alice will be pleased to see you again too. She sure did appreciate your help yesterday."

"She did?" Ava asked, "I thought she was mad at first, but then she gave me a soda and said if anyone was to be in her way, she liked it when they helped her."

Cal chuckled. "My Alice." He looked to Ally in apology. "Always the subtle one."

"We appreciated her letting Ava play with the puppies. We'll just wait outside for you guys to finish up."

Hayes walked towards the door with them. "Why don't we just head on over to the diner? It's not far from here. My brothers clearly have everything under control. Then again, I could do what little brothers do best and butt in with my own opinion, just to muddy the waters a bit more." He wriggled his eyebrows at the thought and Ally grinned.

"That might get a bit scary."

"True. I'd hate to taint Ava's opinion of Graham. He'd turn full on bully if I attempted to thwart his numbers. Come on, they won't miss us." He held open the door without even a glance back at his brothers as they continued to agonize over percentages.

"What is it you will actually be spraying?" Ally asked.

"Skunks?" Ava asked.

Hayes laughed. "Afraid not. We're not that exciting. We'll be spraying brush. Mostly cactus and mesquite."

"What for?" Ava asked.

"Well, several reasons actually," Hayes explained. "We spray the brush now, let it die, and then we'll do a big burn in a few months."

"As in set it on fire?" Ally asked as she reached for Ava's hand to cross the street.

"Yep." Hayes smiled. "Burning is one of our favorite things to do on the ranch. We only do it about every seven years or so though."

"And why burn the pretty grass?" Ava asked.

"It's not really about burning the grass, but more about the brush. Burning kills that. Helps control the spread of pesky cacti and mesquite that take up space in our pastures. We want grass, not brush. And a burn rejuvenates the forage. It cycles nutrients back into the soil and helps us grow even more grass than before. Come spring, we'll have the best lookin' pastures in west Texas." He winked down at Ava as they stepped onto the porch of Sloppy's Diner.

A man so anchored in a wooden chair beside the door, he seemed to be entwined amongst its legs, looked up with a toothless grin. "Well now," He shook Hayes's hand, "I didn't know you left that ranch anymore, horse man."

"Good to see ya, Randy."

"Got you a pretty reason to come to town now, I guess." Randy looked Ally and Ava over and with a satisfied tick of the tongue gave Hayes a solid nod. "Best get them some good eatin'. Sloppy's got the fryer goin'."

"Will do. Take care of yourself now." Hayes patted the man on the shoulder as he held the door open for Ally. "That's Roughneck Randy. He seems a bit..."

"Rough?" Ally supplied.

"Exactly." Hayes chuckled. "But he's got a heart of gold."

She liked that Hayes could look past the man's harsh exterior. And when they walked inside to the smell of freshly fried food tinged with a sweet vanilla smell promising a dessert afterwards, Ally found she looked forward to sharing a meal with Hayes and his brothers more than she realized. He greeted several other townspeople on their way through the restaurant, and he tossed a wave to Ruby, the pretty dark-haired woman from the other day, as they headed towards a table at the back of the diner. Alice sat, a large glass of sweet tea in front of her as Seth and Lawrence bowed their heads over her phone and grimaced at whatever footage she was showing them.

"What are we missing?" Hayes asked.

"The miracle of birth." Lawrence looked up and shimmied his shoulders as if grossed out by what was on the small screen. "As told by a goat, delivering twins... with Alice's help."

"You recorded it?" Hayes asked.

"Why not? It's not every day a goat has twins." Alice welcomed Ava and Ally with a broad smile. "Fancy seeing you two here. Pull up a seat."

"Hi Dr. Alice." Ava sat next to her and pointed to her phone. "Can I see your video?"

Alice looked to Ally and clicked her screen. "I have something better to show you." She tapped on her photo library and pictures of the yellow Labrador puppies filled her screen. "It's Hay!"

"Yep."

"Hay?" Hayes looked up. "You need something, butter bean?"

"No." Ava giggled and turned the phone for him to see the picture of the puppy. "I named this puppy, Hay, like you."

Ally watched as Hayes's eyes softened and he placed a hand over his heart. "Well, now, that is the nicest thing anyone's ever done for me."

Ava waved away his comment and went back to swiping through photos on Alice's phone with the doc's help.

Ally caught Hayes' gaze and flashed a shy smile. "She insisted she name one after you. That one happened to be her favorite. She's asked me three times if we can get the puppy for ourselves."

"And?" Hayes asked.

"Oh, we couldn't." Ally shook her head adamantly. "Our apartment complex doesn't allow pets, and with me being gone all day anyway, it would be hard to take care of one right now."

"I have a puppy. Well, I guess she's not a small puppy anymore, but Cal found some puppies dumped on the side of the road several months ago. Turns out they're pretty good dogs. And I like having the company at the house."

"Ava would love a dog. I debated on whether or not to rent a house for that purpose, instead of an apartment, but the cost of living in Sheffield was just too expensive. Hopefully in the future we'll be able to rent a small place with a yard so she can have a pet. I think it would be good for her. So, what's her name?"

"Her?" Hayes asked.

"Your dog. You said it was a she, right?"

"Oh." He smiled. "Yes. Her name is Yegua."

"Yegua?" Ally asked on a laugh.

"Yep. She's with me at the stables most days, so she might as well fit in."

"But she's a dog."

"And?"

"You can't name a dog 'Horse'."

"Why not?"

She laughed again and had the others looking down the table in their direction. "Estas loco."

"Well, Yegua doesn't mind being named Horse in Spanish. It has a nice ring to it. It also helps her fit in around the stables. And for the record, I am not crazy." They held each other's attention a moment longer as she realized she'd spoken Spanish to him in the midst of her good humor and he'd actually understood her. "And on top of all that, I like it."

"Do you know much Spanish?" Ally asked.

Hayes waved his hand back and forth. "A little bit. Not as much as I'd like. Surprisingly, Lawrence is the most fluent. We attribute that to the fact he just likes to talk a lot."

"I heard that," Lawrence called from down the table, his attention not even focused their direction, but still warranting a response from him.

"But I try. I'm assuming you speak it fluently since you so gracefully did so just now."

"I do."

"And does Ava?"

"Not much, sadly. She knows a bit from when we lived with my parents, but we don't speak it at home much with just the two of us."

"Where do your parents live?"

"El Paso."

"Wow, so you moved from El Paso to Sheffield?"

"Yes."

"That's a change, I'm sure."

"It has been. Not a bad one, though. It's just that we've been in Sheffield for about two years now and I still feel like we are finding our footing."

"Why Sheffield?" Hayes asked.

"I was offered a job at a salon there, before Sandy's. My mother had a friend of a friend, so to speak, and it seemed worth trying out. I was wanting to leave El Paso and it was the first opportunity." She could tell he was curious as to her reasoning for her move, but his interrogation was interrupted by Graham, Calvin, and Philip walking up still arguing about chemicals.

"Give it a rest," Lawrence chided.

"We just got here," Cal stated.

"But I can already tell you three have been at it for the last hour. You get quiet, Philip gets flushed, and Graham gets whiney."

"I do not get whiney," Graham's voice thundered down the table and Lawrence tilted his head in disbelief.

"Oh really?" he baited.

"Oh, stop picking on him, Lawrence." A woman's voice fluttered towards them as she elegantly walked towards the table in a fitted business skirt and flouncy white top. She bent down and kissed Philip sweetly on the lips before sliding into her chair next to him. Her face lit into a welcoming smile as she extended her hand towards Ally. "I'm Helena Shaw."

"Alejandra Garcia."

"Nice to meet you. I've heard about you and your little girl from Julia and Alice. It's nice to finally meet you. I hear Julia's roped you into hair and makeup for portraits and the big day."

"Well, for portraits, yes. She hasn't mentioned the actual wedding day yet."

"Haven't I?" Julia walked up to the table and rested a hand on Graham's shoulder as she greeted everyone with a tired wave. She leaned down and started to kiss Graham but paused. "What's the matter?"

"Nothing."

"Something is the matter." She looked to the other faces at the table.

"Graham's got his panties in a twist over the fact Cal beat him to Philip's earlier," Lawrence explained.

"Um, little ears," Ruby scolded as she swooped behind them to deliver several baskets of onion rings on the table as appetizers. She scurried away faster than a mouse.

Lawrence sent a look of apology in Ally's direction. Ava, thankfully, was completely oblivious, as Alice was now educating her on the different forms of kennel cough she'd come across in all her years of being a veterinarian.

Graham turned his face up to receive the kiss Julia had delayed by her inquisition. She smiled before placing a tender kiss on his lips. "Hi." She hesitated a moment, the two holding each other's gaze a lengthy moment that held more intimacy than Ally'd ever experienced in her entire life. She wondered what that must feel like to have such a relationship. To have that one person you could sink into and find safety, security, and most importantly, love.

Lawrence stood to his feet. "Ruby Cole!" he yelled in a panicked voice across the restaurant. Ruby's head popped up behind the counter as she climbed back to her feet. Lawrence rushed her direction and helped her the remaining way up to find her footing.

"I spilled a drink and slipped." She massaged a sore spot on her elbow and Lawrence gently rubbed his thumb over it.

Julia's hand rested over her heart. "He scared me."

They all watched as Lawrence, satisfied Ruby was okay, walked back towards the table. Kara rushed out of the kitchen with her hands full of plates and began carrying them their direction.

Seth straightened in his chair as she slid his plate in front of him. "Thanks, Kara. This looks delicious."

"You have Sal to thank for that." She grinned as she noticed Philip's empty beer. "Another one, Phil?"

"I'm good, thanks. I think I'll just finish my water."

Helena held up her finger to Kara. "When you have a minute, could I get a tea?"

"Sure thing." Kara smiled. "Anyone else? Everyone else ready to order?" She pulled out a pad and began writing down everyone's order. "I'll have all of this out in two shakes of a lamb's tail." She buzzed away and Ava's brow furrowed.

"A lamb's tail? I don't want a lamb's tail."

Hayes and Calvin chuckled at her reply, and Ally attempted to explain that she would indeed receive her macaroni and cheese and not any part of a lamb.

"You're good at that," Hayes complimented.

"At what?"

"Explaining things to her. I was drawing a blank as to how to even convey what that meant."

"You get used to explaining things, I guess. I feel like that's what I do most days."

"If I'd known I'd be meeting you two for supper I would have brought Ava's bracelet with me," Julia smirked. "I guess you'll still have to come to the ranch this weekend."

Hayes looked to his future sister-in-law and inwardly promoted her to favorite human being in all the world. "This weekend?"

"I invited Ally and Ava out." Julia ran a hand through her dark hair and relaxed in her chair against the arm Graham draped across the back. His thumb absentmindedly rubbed small circles against her shoulder.

"More makeup?" Hayes asked.

Julia shook her head. "No. Just fun."

His eyes lit up and focused upon Ally and she felt her heart do a small flip. "A perfect opportunity for some riding then." He motioned his head towards Ava and Ally nibbled her bottom lip.

"I'm not sure."

"If you're nervous about it and prefer her not to, I understand."

Ally looked towards her daughter as she giggled at a goofy Lawrence making faces through his water glass. The Hastings had been wonderful since meeting them, and if an opportunity for Ava to ride a horse, even for just a moment presented itself, Ally knew she needed to take it. She could never afford riding lessons for her daughter, but Ava loved horses. Perhaps a brief ride on one would satisfy her longing for a horse just a smidgen and give her a wonderful memory. "Alright. But just for a bit."

Hayes clapped his hands and smiled. "I know just the horse too."

Julia placed a sisterly hand on Hayes' shoulder. "And she'll have the best teacher there to help her."

Hayes flushed from her compliment, and Ally liked that he was humble about his gift and skill.

"I guess we will see you and Yegua on Saturday, then."

Hayes beamed across the table. "And who knows? Maybe I'll even get you in a saddle." He winked and her skin warmed, sending a soft tinge of pink to her cheeks.

"Maybe so."

H

Chapter Six

"**She's lookin' mighty pretty** this mornin'." Clint tapped a hand against Vivica's hide and slid his fingers through her mane. "Mighty pretty." The horse preened under his attention and he gently rested his cheek against hers, as if they were old friends.

"I figured if Ally and Ava were going to ride, Vivica would be the best choice. She likes get all dolled up." Hayes walked a saddle over to the horse and draped it across Vivica's back, circling around to pull the straps underneath her girth.

"You seem awfully attentive to that little girl." Clint leaned against the stall door and watched his brother do what he did best. "And her momma."

Hayes shrugged. "Just tryin' to be nice."

"Mm hm. That why she brought you a hot dinner the other day?"

"How did you— nevermind." Hayes shook his head at his brother's meddling. "It was a thank you gift. Nothing more."

"And then she joined us at Sloppy's... on *your* invitation," Clint continued, tallying on his finger's Hayes' extra attention.

"Do you have a point you're gettin' at, Clint?" Irked, Hayes slid the bridle over Vivica's ears.

"Four of us have fallen in love in the last year, Hayes. Four. By now, I've seen how it starts, and the way you're doting on that hairdresser and her daughter, I'd say you're well on the way to being the next one."

"So, because I'm being nice to someone, I must be falling in love? That's ridiculous. Besides, I don't even know Ally that well. I literally just met her and her daughter. Just because I see a way I can help her and Ava, doesn't mean I'm planning on matrimony. Besides, I don't have much to offer a woman these days."

"Much to offer?" Calvin's voice drifted into the barn as he strode in and tossed Clint his keys. "That is to the ATV. Give it a spin and let me know how it rides. We'll be using it for sprayin'."

KATHARINE E. HAMILTON

Clint nodded and headed out of the barn. "What was that all about?"

Hayes grumbled beneath his breath and then shook away the beginnings of a tainted mood. "Clint just has it in his head that I'm fallin' in love with Alejandra."

Calvin leaned against Vivica and rested her head on his shoulder as he looked to his younger brother while he prepped the stall for when Vivica would return after a long ride. "And are you?"

"What?" Hayes's head popped up. "No. That's absurd."

"Why?"

"As I explained to Clint, no."

Cal smiled. "Okay. Well, I just came by to give Clint the keys. You set for starting to spray tomorrow?"

"I thought you and Clint were doing that?"

"We are. But I'm going to need a reliever at some point."

"Gotcha. Yeah, just let me know when. I'm just going to be working on breaking the bronc this week."

"Alright." Cal walked back towards the sunlight and Hayes followed.

"How are you getting back to your place?"

"Not headed to my place."

"Where you headed?"

"To Graham's."

"Is he there?"

"Oh yes, poring over the budget."

"Fun stuff. Sorry I'm missing out."

"I bet you are. You enjoy giving rides to pretty ladies while I number crunch with our brother."

"I appreciate your sacrifices, Cal."

Laughing, Cal started trudging up the dirt road that would wind him back towards the main road and on up to Graham's house. He waved over his shoulder.

Hayes turned his attention back to the barn and as he was about to walk back inside, Julia's car pulled to a brief stop to chat with Calvin on the road before heading his direction. Her passengers, Ally and Ava, were both riding shotgun, Ava sitting in Ally's lap. Julia pulled to a stop and hopped out, her hair tied back in a ponytail, her face void of any makeup. She was still one of the prettiest women Hayes had ever seen. Graham was blessed. Ally stepped out, her long, dark hair draped over her shoulder in a thick braid that reached almost to her waist, uncertain eyes, and worn cowboy boots. Intrigued, he wondered why she even owned a pair. Ava, dressed in jeans and a sparkly pink button up, looked the part of rodeo princess, and he couldn't help but smile at the two of them.

"Mornin'," he greeted with a warm wave, and Ava rushed towards him, already talking and excited to see his horses.

"I hear ya, butter bean. I'll introduce you to all of them here shortly. I promise." He removed his hat as Ally stepped forward and he nodded a formal greeting to her and Julia before slapping it back on his head. "You ladies ready to ride?"

"I am not today," Julia reported. "Graham is here, and I don't want him to see me." She leaned towards Ally. "It's a surprise for him. Hayes is sweet enough to help me conquer my fear of horses so that I can ride around the ranch with Graham again one day soon. Today, I am just an audience."

"Those are welcome too," Hayes encouraged. "Come on into my domain." He waved them forward, Ava grabbing his work-rough hand and swinging it back and forth as he led her inside. He winked down at her and stopped her a few feet in front of Vivica.

"Wow! A horse! Momma, look!"

"I see."

Hayes squatted beside Ava and pointed up at Vivica. "Now, a few rules before we get started. There's always rules when it comes to animals, especially animals that are bigger than us."

"Okay."

"First, we try to talk real soft like when inside the barn. Loud noises can sometimes make them nervous."

"I'll be soft," she promised with wide eyes.

He smirked. "Good. Rule number two is you have to listen to everything I say. You cannot wander around without me. And you cannot touch anything without asking first. Got it?"

"Yes sir." She nodded solemnly, her little hands already itching to touch Vivica.

"Rule number three," He paused until she looked him in the eye. "have fun."

She hopped up and down and nodded.

"Alright, now, let me show you how to walk up to a horse." He guided her toward Vivica, and Ava began talking in sweet tones of adoration as she was allowed to pet the horse. Vivica gave answering snorts that only encouraged the little girl further.

"Look, Momma, she's my new best friend."

Julia chuckled next to her. "Vivica is the horse Hayes has been teaching me on. She's very docile."

"Good." Ally held an anxious hand to her heart. "I have to admit I'm a little nervous."

"Hayes is a wonderful teacher. If you're at all uncomfortable, just tell him."

"Alright, Momma," He waved towards Ally. "your turn."

Ally hesitantly walked forward, and he gently grabbed her hand and placed it on Vivica's snout. "Just let her get to know you a bit."

Ava stood proudly next to Vivica, her hands already holding onto the reins as if her post were most important.

"I figured," Hayes murmured towards her. "I'd get in the saddle and have you hand her up to me. You okay with that? Or would you prefer to be up in the saddle with her?"

Ally shook her head. "Let her start with you."

"Alright." Hayes knelt beside Ava. "Okay, Ava, here's the plan. You're going to ride with me first."

Giddy, Ava bounced from side to side. "Okay."

"I need those." He pointed to the reins, and she handed them to him immediately. He nodded towards Ally and she stepped forward to help with

Ava as he hoisted himself into the saddle. Vivica shifted under his weight. He draped the reins how he liked them and then reached his arms down. Ally lifted her daughter up to him and Ava slid into the front of the saddle, her hands on the saddle horn. He looked down at Ally to make sure she was okay with Ava up in the saddle. "Ready?"

Ally hesitated a moment but nodded. "Alright, butter bean, here we go. You just hold onto the saddle horn there, and I'll get us movin'." He grabbed the reins and lightly clicked his heels into Vivica's flanks. The horse lumbered forward at a slow pace, Ava gasping in glee as they exited the barn. Julia and Ally followed as Hayes led the horse into the pens. Julia closed the gate behind them, and she and Ally leaned against the fence railing to watch as he led Ava and Vivica slowly around the pens.

"He's so patient with all of her questions." Ally listened as Ava talked a thousand words a minute to a relaxed Hayes.

"Hayes is a great listener. I haven't known the brothers that long, but in the months that I have, Hayes is the one most go to if they need a listening ear. He's a sweetheart." Julia waved as they turned their direction to circle around the fence. Ava raised a hand and waved towards them, her face split into a joyous smile. She pointed her free hand to the other that Hayes had allowed to help hold one of the reins and the women smiled.

"She's in heaven." Ally laughed as her daughter went right back into conversation, the lingering words of "and my teacher" drifting towards them. "He'll know everything about us by the end of this."

"Kids are great." Julia sighed in contentment as the breeze teased her hair. "I hope Graham and I can bring some little ones to the place soon."

"Do you want seven?" Ally asked.

"Heavens, no." Julia laughed. "But I certainly want a brood. Graham is of the same mind, so I imagine we will work on starting a family right off. I may have to pick your brain if we end up having a little girl. I'm not sure Graham would know what to do."

Ally chuckled. "That's the lovely thing about little girls, they just come out telling you what to do."

"Heaven help us if there is a Hastings baby girl." Julia turned with a sparkle in her eyes as Hayes pulled up beside them and halted.

∞

"One rider down. Second rider ready?" Hayes asked Ally.

Her heart thundered in her chest as Hayes dismounted and reached up for Ava. Her little girl dove willingly into his arms and he aided her in climbing over the fence. "Do it, Momma! Do it!"

Julia chuckled at Ava's enthusiasm as Ally swung her legs over the fence and her boots touched the dirt on the other side. "Now or never, I guess."

"I won't make you ride with me," Hayes chuckled as he pointed to the stirrup and for her to lift her boot. She inwardly wished he would ride with her. She wasn't accustomed to such a large animal, and her hands were already sweating. She lifted her boot and slipped it into the stirrup, her hand up on the saddle horn. She inhaled a deep breath and then stopped, releasing her hold and removing her foot. "Wait." She shook her hands by her sides and Hayes gently rested a hand on her lower back. "I won't let you fall, and I won't let go of the reins until you're comfortable enough to do it yourself."

"And if I'm not?"

"Then I'll just lead you around." He flashed an encouraging smile.

"Okay." She wiped her palms on her jeans and then reached up for the saddle horn again, Hayes's strong hands helping her up and into the saddle. Vivica shifted and Ally nervously gripped the horn until the horse steadied.

"How you feel?" Hayes asked, looking up at her, his eyes squinting against the sun.

"Nervous."

"Alright, we'll take it slow. Here we go." He began leading Vivica away from the fence.

"Wait, wait, wait wait." Ally's voice hitched in fear and Hayes immediately stopped the horse's progression. "I don't know if I can do this."

He looked up at her, running a calming hand over the horse's cheek as he spoke. "Want down?"

"I just need a second to... acclimate to being up here."

"Take your time." Hayes continued spoiling the horse and giving Ally space until she exhaled a deep breath. "Okay."

"Alright." He gently tugged on the reins and Vivica moved a few steps forward.

Ally leaned forward.

"Sit up," Hayes instructed. "You'll have better balance."

"I can't." Ally's voice grew faint as she felt her heartbeat explode in her chest. She'd had anxiety attacks before; it'd been a problem over the last decade. But to have one on the back of a horse would not only be a disaster, but new. Typically, her triggers were enclosed spaces or an overwhelming sense of fear. She wasn't scared of horses. She wasn't scared of heights, but something wasn't right, and she felt her vision speckle. "I need to get down. Necesito bajar ahora."

Her words rushed out and Hayes stopped the horse and barely made it to the side of the horse to catch a falling Ally as she struggled to remove herself from the saddle in a hurry. She felt his arms come around her and save her from busting her rear on the ground.

"Easy, easy." His breath teased her hair as he held her tight, his arms secure. "Take a breath."

"Lo estoy intentando," she panted, placing a hand on her heart.

"Do you need to sit?" Hayes asked, his tone never wavering or growing frustrated.

"Momma?" Ava's voice sounded worried, and Julia placed a calming hand on Ava's shoulder.

"I'm fine. Estoy bien," she assured her daughter. She turned towards Hayes, his grip never leaving her, causing them to be in one another's arms. She rested her hands on his forearms and avoided his gaze. Her breathing slowed and she felt her heart returning to its normal rhythm. "Estoy bien," she whispered, not only for him to hear, but to convince herself. His hold relaxed and he released her. "Again," she said and turned to face the horse.

"You sure?" Hayes asked, surprise raising his brows up under his hat.

"Yes. The only way to conquer a fear is to keep trying. Am I right, mija?" Ally looked to Ava and her daughter gave a pleased and affirmative nod.

Impressed, Hayes smiled. "Okay."

"Only this time, I'd like you to ride with me." Ally caught his calm blue gaze and he nodded. He helped her into the saddle and her heart started its hammering, but before it zoomed out of control, she felt Hayes's presence behind her, and his arms slip around her to grab the reins. Instant relief had her relaxing in the saddle, and instead of leaning forward, she felt herself pressing back against Hayes's embrace a bit more than was necessary. He clicked the reins and slowly guided them away from the fence. The horse's movements were methodic, rhythmic, and not as scary as she first thought.

"Want to trot?" Hayes asked, his voice low beside her ear. She felt a tingle drift down her spine and into her arms at the feeling of his breath on her ear and nodded. Her hands moved from the saddle horn to his forearms as he held onto the reins and guided Vivica at a steadier pace around the pens. Her braid bounced against her chest and she found herself smiling as the wind brushed against her face. Before she knew it, they'd halted by the fence and she was opening her eyes to a proud daughter.

"You were glorious." Julia clapped her hands in cheer as Ava bounced excitedly next to her.

Hayes dismounted and then reached up to help her down, his hands on her waist. She turned when her boots hit the ground and wrapped her arms around his neck. Her actions took him by surprise—she could tell by his quick step back to affirm his footing— but he accepted the hug in kind, and when she pulled away, he tipped his hat. "Thank you."

"My pleasure." He led Vivica back towards the fence and tied her reins.

Ava hugged Ally's legs in a tight embrace, and both glowed with accomplishment as well as thrill.

"I think this calls for some celebratory ice cream," Julia said. "I started a batch of peach ice cream up at the house. Hayes, will you join us?"

"Well, I—"

"Please do," Ally invited, her eyes searching his as he rubbed a hand over the back of his neck, weighing his options of escape, no doubt. Disappointment welled inside of her at not getting to spend more time with him, but it was clear he was ready to be rid of them for the day.

"If you're worried about Graham and Calvin, they'll be done with the budget, so you won't be roped into it," Julia reported.

Hayes's expression lifted considerably, and Ally realized he was only avoiding his older brothers and not her invitation. "Then I guess I could make some room for peach ice cream. Though, if we play football later and I'm miserable, I'm going to blame the three of you. Let me take Vivica back, and I'll meet you up at the house."

"I'll take Ava with me to help finish up the ice cream," Julia suggested. "Why don't you show Ally a bit more of the ranch on your way back." She tugged the little girl towards her car, and they were already headed up the road before Ally and Hayes could even muster a response.

"Well, I had planned to ride Flash up to the house, but I can grab my truck from the house." Hayes pointed towards the horizon, but Ally didn't see anything. He walked Vivica into her stall, unsaddled her, and brushed her coat before draping the saddle in its designated spot on the wall. "It's a bit of a walk. That alright?"

"Sure." Ally followed him out of the barn and up a separate road leading towards the horizon he'd just pointed at. "I live a bit further out than the rest of them," Hayes explained. "Where it's quiet."

"It's a beautiful ranch. I doubt there's a bad spot anywhere. One thing about living with my parents for a few years, there was always noise. Now that it's just Ava and me, we've grown accustomed to the quiet."

"Do you have Ava full time?" Hayes asked curiously.

"Yes." Ally was used to the question, but it was still so hard to answer that she'd failed Ava in such a grave way. "Her father isn't in her life."

"I'm sorry to hear that," Hayes replied. "But sometimes it's for the best. I hope that's the case for you two."

"It is." Thankful for his nonjudgmental response, Ally looked him over as they walked. "And thank you."

"For what?"

"Not offering advice or commentary about the importance of a father in a young girl's life."

"People actually do that?" He looked baffled.

"All the time."

"I hate hearing that. You're her mother, you know what's best for her. Clearly, Ava is happy and taken care of. So, I'd say you've been doing a good job. And I'm not a parent, so I have no advice or grounds to offer any alternative lifestyle suggestions. Nor is it my place. That's crazy that people feel like they can do that."

"I've gotten used to it. I just keep my mouth shut and know they mean well."

"Still... can't be easy."

"It's not. But I do my best. And it's not that I don't agree with the people. In a perfect world, I would love for her to have a father who loves her and cares for her. But this world is far from perfect, and sometimes we have to choose a different path."

"I understand that. We lost both our parents. Not exactly how you envision life. But we thank the Lord every day for Annie and Henry. They stepped in when they didn't have to, and now we love them as if they were our parents. You never know who God will place in your life when you need them most. At least, that's what's happened around here. Julia being another example. Graham was and *is* a hard man. He's always been tough. I guess he's always felt the pressure of being the head of the family after our parents passed. Anyway, Julia shows up out of the blue, sweeps him off his feet, and now, life is different. Better. Graham is better. She only makes him stronger. But if you would have asked any of us if we envisioned Graham being in love or getting married, we would have laughed. But... his path took a turn. Unexpectedly, but in a great way. I hope that your path has been good despite the challenges I'm sure you've faced." His hand swooped out and blocked her from continuing forward. "Stay back."

Her gaze flashed to the ground in front of them. A few feet away was a rattle snake, curled around itself, sunning in the dirt path.

"Serpiente. Ay no." Ally took two steps back behind Hayes.

"I'd say we leave him be, but we can't get around him where he's at." He looked around and reached into the brush, retrieving a long stick. He tested its strength and then began to step forward.

Ally grabbed his free hand. "Hayes, no. Are you crazy?"

He smirked and squeezed her hand. "I'll be fine. Common occurrence around here. Just need to give him a little nudge and send him on his way." He kicked a few rocks in the direction of the snake and it immediately uncurled and scurried into the brush.

"But it's free?"

"Yep."

"You just let it free?"

"Well, it's not exactly an aggressor to things bigger than it is. Typically, we only kill them if they come up near the houses, barns, or troughs."

Ally hesitated a moment as Hayes continued on his way. He turned back around, and his lips twitched. "It's gone. Trust me." He extended his hand towards her and she ignored the offer, but high stepped over where the snake had once been.

"I don't like snakes."

"Really? I could hardly tell."

She lightly jabbed his shoulder as he chuckled, and they cleared the top of the hill. His house, a nice brick and stone combination, sat nestled amongst some large oak trees. A dog barked and sprinted in their direction. He accepted the dog's excited licks and jumps. "Down, Yegua. Down." He ruffled her ears and then looked up at Ally. "This is my girl."

"She's beautiful."

"I think so too." Hayes gave his dog a quick kiss on the head and she fell into loyal step beside him. She acknowledged Ally with a cursory glance but kept to her main man's side.

"You have a beautiful house."

"Thanks."

"It looks new."

"A couple of years." Hayes walked to the metal shed next to the house and opened the door. I don't drive my truck much, so it will appreciate getting some sun."

"Do you not drive it around the ranch?"

"Not usually. I'm either on a horse or a piece of equipment. And I don't go to town much."

"And still despite that, you have a reputation." Ally hopped into the passenger side of his truck and closed the door.

"A reputation? What kind of reputation?" Hayes asked.

The corners of her mouth tilted as she turned towards him. "You and your brothers have a reputation of being some of the most eligible bachelors in the area."

He flushed. "Oh."

"I've been privy to many a conversation at the hair salon where the female population wonders how they can go about meeting a Hastings brother."

"That's... interesting."

She laughed at his uncomfortable shift in his seat as he cranked the engine to life. "And actually, about the time one of those conversations was happening, in waltzed you and Philip. To say that quieted the room would be an understatement."

"I wondered why they all stared at us. Now I just feel weird."

She grinned at him as he rubbed a hand over his face to cover his embarrassed smile. "You should."

His confused expression made her laugh even harder. "I'm kidding."

Relief flooded his face as he backed out of the shed and headed towards Graham's house. It was only a couple of miles, but the silence that lingered between them held warmth and ease. "Thanks for today, Hayes. Once I overcame my anxiety, I enjoyed riding Vivica. And I know for a fact Ava was in heaven."

"You're welcome." He turned his sweet gaze towards her before a small frown of disappointment crossed his face upon arriving at his brother's house. All of his brothers graced the front porch of Graham's house with bowls of ice cream.

"What's the matter?" Ally placed a hand on his arm in concern and he briefly looked down at her touch.

"Nothing. I'm just dreading getting whipped in football today."

"Football?"

"Every Saturday here at Graham's. I've been on the losing team three weeks in a row. My *reputation* is that I'm a curse on the field."

She smiled. "I think you'll do great today."

"Oh yeah? Why's that?"

"Because I'm here to cheer you on. And Ava. We won't let you down."

He patted her hand. "I guess if I have fans, I should definitely kick it into gear, then. Come on, let's get some of that ice cream."

H

Chapter Seven

"*Trisket looks fancy.*" Seth patted Graham's horse as Hayes tucked the bridle over Trisket's ears and led her out of the barn.

"She has to look good today for Julia's photo op."

"I hate to break it to you, Trisket," Seth chatted. "But as pretty as you are today, ain't nobody gonna look better than Julia."

Trisket, as if she'd been offended, turned her head to nuzzle Hayes' shoulder instead of Seth's. Hayes absentmindedly patted her cheek as they continued walking.

"Here comes Al and Cal." Seth pointed up the road as their older brother and Alice pulled up near the barn.

Alice opened the door and stood on the running board. "You going to take all day? Julia's already up on the hill waiting. Photographer too. Hurry up!" She hopped back in the truck and they drove on past.

"She's so bossy," Seth muttered and had Hayes laughing.

"We need a bossy woman sometimes. Why don't you go on ahead? Trisket and I will be there soon. I don't want to rush her so she's not sweaty."

"Got it." Seth tipped his hat at the command and jogged over to the UTV he'd driven up to the barn.

Hayes, enjoying the quiet and the steady rhythm of Trisket's hooves, continued on at a leisurely pace. He wouldn't be late. He wouldn't postpone photos by taking his time. In fact, he was sure everyone was working hard on setting up the photo site and hadn't even noticed he wasn't there yet. Except Alice. The quiet moments on the ranch were his favorite. It was why he enjoyed living the farthest out, why he secluded himself at the stables and barn, and why he rarely ventured into town. He liked solitude. He liked taking time to soak in the place. His blood, sweat, and tears had literally gone into the very soil he walked on, and he reveled in it. His commitment to the ranch was bone deep and taking a few minutes to breathe it in each day rejuvenated that love for the land. Graham understood. He was the same way. Cal, though he leaned more towards machines than animals, loved the place. Lawrence, though not one to harp on the subject, felt extreme loyalty to the place and the lifestyle it provided. It wouldn't be long before Ruby joined him on the ranch, and they'd start their own family. Philip loved the ranch in his own way. Though he'd never commit fully to working the place, his thoughts had begun churning on building a house amongst the rest of them. Helena was to thank for that. Clint, well, he was still floundering a bit, but he had his mind set on hunting. His early planning stages for a hunting operation on the place were impressive. Hayes knew it was only a matter of time and that ball would start rolling and Clint would succeed. But Seth... the youngest brother seemed to be following in Graham's steps. He had leadership potential. Though he wished to one day hold more responsibility on the place, Seth was still a bit wet behind the ears when standing amongst his brothers. But his commitment didn't waver. He took his lot as a challenge. He continually tried to prove himself and do the best work he could, and he did it mostly with a positive attitude. Hayes' brothers were all different and unique in personality and strengths, but as he crested the hill and saw all of them but Graham standing about a gorgeous Julia in her white flowing dress, they all looked the same. Dumbstruck and grinning, he halted Trisket next to Philip and turned his attention to the beautiful bride-to-be.

"Oh good, Trisket is here." Her eyes lit in gratitude as she lifted the ends of her dress and walked towards the horse. "She looks beautiful, Hayes, thank you."

"As do you. I think I'm speechless."

She blushed at his compliment and tucked a stray whisp of hair behind her ear as the wind sent a small breeze over the crowd.

"Alright, folks." The photographer, a hip mid-twenties blonde bombshell named Stacy, motioned for everyone to come towards her. "We're starting here on the hill with a few shots of Julia by herself, then a few with the horse, and then with the group of you brothers. After that, she said she has a couple of other spots she'd like portraits taken. We need to move rather quickly because of the sunlight. Right now, we have decent cloud coverage which will lend itself to perfect lighting. Now, let's get her set up." Stacy pointed her finger to a spot and Julia made her way there. Alice knelt and spread her dress around her as Ally lightly dusted Julia's nose with powder and then fixed the fly-away strands of her hair.

Hayes watched in wonder as the women worked. "Who knew so much went into bridal portraits? Annie not here?"

"Henry had a last minute hip twinge. She took him into Fort Stockton to make sure his hip replacement wasn't having issues. She texted a bit ago that all was fine," Philip whispered. "And yeah, it's interesting being on this side of things. Maybe Julia is teaching us all a lesson."

"What do you mean?"

"She's showing us the inside scoop so that one day when our time comes, we'll appreciate the effort behind the beauty."

Hayes chuckled. "Possibly. Though I think you're closer to worrying about that than I am."

"True."

Hayes's mouth dropped open. "Wait, what? I was kiddin'."

Philip laughed. "Well, I'm not. I'd be a fool not to swoop Helena up. I'm just waiting for the right moment."

"Wow." Hayes watched as the photographer directed Julia's movements, the other women swooping in between shots to refresh hair and dress. "First Graham, then Cal, then you, and Lawrence next. Is this catching?" Hayes took a step away from his brother and Philip playfully shoved him two more.

"For your sake, I hope it is."

"Why's that?"

"Because there's nothing better than having the love of a good woman."

"Are you about to start singing?"

Philip rolled his eyes. "No. I'll leave that to Lawrence."

They watched as their brother whistled the wedding march to make Julia smile.

"Horse!" the photographer yelled.

"Wow, she's about as bad as Alice," Hayes murmured.

Philip grinned as Hayes led Trisket towards Julia.

"Watch the dress, watch the dress." The photographer pointed and looked through her lens several times before holding a hand up. "Stop. Right there."

"Do you want the bridle on?" Hayes asked.

"No. Take it off," Stacy ordered.

Hayes gently removed the bridle and smoothed out Trisket's mane. "She'll be a good girl for ya, Jewels."

Julia nodded her thanks as the photographer gave her orders on poses. Hayes stepped back and bumped into Ally. He jumped and sidestepped. "Sorry about that."

"No worries." She held a bag over her shoulder that had tiny plastic drawers on the side and brushes tucked into pockets.

"Makeup to go?"

She giggled. "Something like that."

"Where's Ava?" Hayes looked around.

"She's at school. I didn't want her to get in the way today."

"Well, it's always good to see you."

"You too."

He felt her studying his side profile and turned. "What?"

"You're all cleaned up for pictures. I don't think I've ever seen you—" She trailed off.

"Clean?" He laughed. "I'm not offended by the observation."

She smiled. "Yeah, I guess that's what I was going to say. You clean up nice."

He tilted his head towards her, and his lips tilted in a lopsided smile. "Thanks. I try every once in a while. Besides, I was under strict orders to look my best today."

"A lot goes into bridal pictures."

"Tell me about it. I had no idea."

"I'm thankful Julia hired me for such an occasion. It will really help build my business having her in my portfolio."

"She's a beautiful bride. Graham's heart's going to stop when he sees her."

"That's sweet."

"You ever been married?" Hayes asked.

She shook her head, her eyes dropping to her feet a moment.

"That's a shame," he said. "I bet you'd paint a pretty picture all done up and in white too."

"Not sure that's in the cards for me," Ally replied.

"Never know. Lord knows I never thought my brothers would be thinking of matrimony. And not only Graham, but Lawrence, and just talking to Phil, it sounds like he may be the next one to pop the question. We're droppin' like flies around here."

She chuckled. "Is that a bad thing?"

"Not at all. Just surprising. We've all been out here keepin' to ourselves and then all of a sudden, women just start poppin' up in our lives left and right, and we lose our senses."

"There's still three of you who haven't fallen victim to the L word."

"True. I'm not sure if it's in the cards for me either."

"Why's that?"

"I'm too much of a loner. She'd have to be one special lady to deal with me and my hermit ways."

"Makeup!" the photographer yelled.

Hayes hissed in displeasure at the woman's call. "She's about to drive me nuts." He walked forward as Ally rushed towards Julia to check hair and makeup as they shifted her towards a different pose. "Ma'am—" Hayes' voice was calm but direct as he addressed the photographer.

"Is there a problem?" she asked, barely glancing his direction as she switched out lenses.

"When you yell, it disturbs the horse, so you might keep the tone on a lower register."

Her head popped up. "Excuse me?"

He could tell his comment frustrated her, but he wasn't about to have a runaway horse, especially since Julia'd worked so hard to overcome her fear. "Just don't want to spook the horse."

"Well, we're done with it, so you can move it anyway."

His back stiffened at her order and she met his gaze straight on, as if challenging him to talk back to her. Hayes made up his mind right then that he didn't like her.

"It's a horse, not an 'it.'" Ally's voice dripped with disdain as the woman turned her direction. Her lips flapped a moment as if she wished to respond, but realized she was currently being paid to take photos for Julia and didn't want to mess up the opportunity. Instead of voicing more of her attitude, she turned and stalked back towards Julia.

Hayes slipped the bridle back on Trisket and rubbed behind her ears. "Looked beautiful, Trisket. Graham will be pleased." The horse snorted in response and accepted the carrot stick Hayes pulled from his back pocket.

"Alright, now we need the men," the photographer called.

"About time!" Lawrence clapped his hands and darted towards Julia. He swept her off her feet and spun her in a circle, despite the worried calls from the other women. He set her back to rights as she laughed and placed a steadying hand on his arm and the other brothers joined them. Hayes handed Trisket's reins to Alice and walked forward, waiting to see where the photographer wished to place him. Philip kissed the back of Julia's hand and Calvin removed his hat as he approached her. The photographer snapped photo after photo of the interaction until everyone began lining up around Julia.

8

"They're a handsome bunch, aren't they?" Alice grinned as Seth was shoved towards the end of the line, but Julia scolded the older brothers and the youngest soon found himself right next to her.

"They are," Ally agreed. When the men had settled, the photographer waved her forward and she hurried towards Julia. She fluffed the dress since Alice's hands were full and then lightly touched up Julia's makeup and hair.

"What about me?" Clint asked.

Ally playfully swiped her makeup brush over his nose and cheeks before stepping back towards Alice.

"Took me almost an hour to iron Cal's shirt. I don't think he's ever done it himself. Annie spoils them." Alice shifted her grip on Trisket's reins as the horse tugged towards Hayes. "Oh, alright." Alice released her hold and Trisket lumbered towards her second favorite brother.

"Uh oh. The photographer isn't going to be happy," Ally muttered.

"Not sure anything could make her happy. Except maybe Clint." Alice pointed to the way the photographer fluffed her hair when Clint began talking to her.

"Huye, Clint, huye," Ally warned.

Alice guffawed, making Ally do the same as Trisket muscled her way into the photo, nudging Philip aside to stand next to Hayes as if she were the star of the photo instead of Julia, which only made the women laugh harder. Ally caught Hayes' amused expression as he lovingly patted Trisket's cheek.

"Okay, I think we are done in this location." The photographer, clearly put out by all the shenanigans, motioned towards her car.

"Where did Julia find this girl?" Ally asked.

"Who knows? All I know is that we are going to have a serious talk about hiring a different photographer for the wedding. This girl is somethin' else."

Hayes and Clint walked towards them. "What's so funny over here?" Clint asked.

"Trisket." Alice rubbed a hand over the horse's snout and grinned. "Diva."

"It was cute she went straight to you." Ally gathered up her various makeup bags, along with the one on her shoulder, and accepted the helping hand Hayes offered in carrying one for her.

"Trisket and I have a special relationship."

"How so?"

"She was the first horse I ever trained, so she holds a piece of my heart."

"I think she knows it too."

"That she does." He smirked as they fell into step alongside each other. Ally could have hitched a ride with Alice or Cal to the next location, but she liked talking with Hayes. And since he was walking the horse, she didn't mind giving him the company.

"Ava has talked nonstop about riding Vivica. Her teacher sent a note home saying she proudly shared her adventure during story time. She never shares anything in class, so that was a huge feat."

"I'm glad." Hayes's soft gaze washed over her before he tossed a wave to Seth and Clint on the buggy as they drove passed them.

"I was going to talk with you about lessons for her. Cost and such. I'm not sure if I could do weekly lessons right now, but maybe we could work something out?"

"For sure. Though I won't be able to start with her for a couple of weeks because I'm on retainer to help with spraying this next week, and I've got to get that bronc settled down and broke. He's eatin' my lunch, and I'm tired of it. Graham's about lost patience with him too, so if I don't get him broken in the next couple of weeks, I'm probably going to have to sell him. And I don't want to."

"Oh, well, it's not a big deal if you can't."

"I want to. Just give me a couple of weeks."

"I don't want you to have to worry ab—"

"Ally," His voice held a sternness she hadn't heard before, and she anxiously looked at him. "I said I would like to teach Ava. And I will. You're not thwarting my schedule or anything. I just need to knock out a couple things first and then I will be able to dedicate the time she will need. And I'm more than happy to do it."

"Okay." She quieted as they rounded the curve of the road and saw the next photo set up taking shape. "Thank you."

"What about you?" he asked.

"Me?"

"Well, if I'm teachin' Ava, I might as well teach you at the same time."

"Oh, I can't really afford the both of us at the moment."

"I thought you said we were going to work something out?"

"For Ava," she reiterated.

"You both need to be in the saddle," Hayes recommended.

"Hayes—" She didn't know how to stress to him how tight her budget was and how little wiggle room she had. Being a single mom was tough, especially when she was still trying to build up her salon clientele.

"It'll be alright, trust me."

"I don't want charity."

"It won't be. You'll earn it. While Ava is training, you can help me with other things around the stalls and barn."

"As in chores?"

"If you're going to learn to ride a horse, you might as well learn how to take care of one too."

She thought it over a minute before deciding his offer was more than fair. "I'm listening."

H

Chapter Eight

Spraying brush was monotonous work, but Hayes didn't mind filling in for a couple of hours while Cal had some lunch and a little rest after being up so early. Though they all had been set back a couple of days prior when they realized Clint hadn't cleaned out the tank and pump from the last spraying job and the chemical had eroded the diaphragm of the pump. Philip ordered the part to replace it and now they were back on track, but Graham's grouchy disposition was set for the week after that. Clint had somewhat redeemed himself by waking up at the crack of dawn this morning to get started on the mesquite in the traps and pens. Calvin had started spraying the cacti in the same areas. They'd eventually push out to the pastures and fence lines, but for now, the pens and traps were the focus. Hayes sprayed the cactus and moved forward in the buggy to spray the next one.

Tedious work but worth it. And if they wanted to burn, it was necessary. With the wedding in the spring, Graham was determined to burn so that the ranch and pastures looked their best for his and Julia's big day. So, the brothers did what they did best, they rallied together to make it happen. Clint, though busy spraying mesquite, would leave in a just a few short months to go to New Mexico for hunting season, determined to work and learn more about a commercial hunting operation, in order to implement that knowledge into his own plans for the 7H. It'd be good for his brother to branch out of Parks. Meanwhile, Hayes would stay here, tend to his horses, help out wherever else was needed, and be ready to burn when Graham gives the say so.

He hadn't called upon Alejandra again the last several days. After the photo shoot, his focus was on breaking horses and spraying. He'd been honest about that with her, but he also didn't want to let too much time pass, or she might change her mind about lessons. He was looking forward to having her and Ava out at the ranch more. He also liked to help when he was needed, and he could tell Ava needed an outlet, a safe haven to just be free and as rambunctious as she wanted. And he could tell Ally was in need of something too, but he couldn't quite put his finger on it. She was a hard one to figure out. He sensed she came from a pretty tough situation in regards to being a single mom and facing the responsibility alone, but there was a wall she hid behind. He could only get to know her so much before he saw her erect the wall and grow quiet. Maybe working with the horses will help her relax and understand he just wants to be her friend. He could tell she enjoyed spending time with all of them, so lessons at the horse pens would give her more reason to hang out with everyone. And him. He tampered down the small touch of interest that threatened to surface when he thought of Ally. He couldn't think along those lines. He was happy with his life the way it was. There was no need for a woman. And Ally deserved a man fully committed to her and Ava. A little girl who had not had a present father needed a man who was ready to take on the role and do it justice. Hayes wasn't sure that was him. He'd never given much thought about kids. Yes, he'd built his house big enough that if he ever did marry and have a family, they'd have room. But it was a passing thought, not one that he'd truly considered important at the time. But now? He sighed as he steered the buggy towards another cacti bunch and sprayed. He wasn't ready for that level of commitment. But when he thought about Ally's dark eyes and hair and the lilt to her laugh, he felt his stance wavering. The way she slipped into speaking Spanish when she was nervous, scared, or excited made him smile, and Ava was the spunkiest little girl he'd ever met and only seemed to make Ally even more appealing in the way she loved her daughter. No more. No more thinking about Ally, Hayes told himself. His focus was on cactus. Cactus. Cactus. Cactus.

"Hayes!" Cal's voice finally drifted to him through the brain fog, and he turned off the buggy to hear what Calvin had to say.

"I've been yellin' at you for five minutes. Didn't you hear me?"

"Sorry, I was lost in my thoughts. You back?"

"Yep. I'll take it over from here."

"Good. I need to get back to the stables. I think I'm going to go for a long ride."

"Hey, while you're at it, check that back fence-line." Cal suggested. "I want to know if we have any holes back there. I'm wanting to clear and repair that here soon, but Graham doesn't seem to think it worthwhile if there aren't many holes."

"The Chandler boundary fence-line?" Hayes asked.

"Yeah. The whole thing if you have time."

"I'll do it. That's a shaded route, so I won't complain." Hayes walked to his truck parked beside the cow pens and waved before heading towards the stable barn.

He saddled up Flash, not because he didn't have other horses that could use some exercise, but he was feeling a bit broody, and the only companion for a good brood was Flash. He didn't have to guide Flash on where to go, the horse's steps knew exactly where Hayes wished to head. At a leisurely pace, they set out behind his house and towards the back property line. Hayes liked riding the Chandler boundary when he had a chance. It was quiet, far removed from the rest of the ranch, and rarely did they move cattle this far out from the main hub. It was a quiet slice of heaven. His house was closest to it, and he felt like he had it all to himself. He'd occasionally set up snares along the fence-line to help with predators, coyotes being the main culprits. He'd snare for a couple of months around the holes and dig outs and then patch them up. Graham didn't ask him to, no one did, but it was something that was necessary, and he didn't mind taking the extra time here and there to check the line.

Flash's ears pricked and slanted back, and Hayes lifted his eyes ahead to see, scattered amongst some of the largest oak and cottonwood trees on the ranch, a herd of elk. Elk weren't common in the area. In fact, they'd never had elk on the 7H. Ever. Though they'd heard rumor of elk showing up in the area, none of them actually believed it. He squinted to make sure it was indeed elk and despite his lack of knowledge in the wildlife arena, much to Clint's disappointment, the animals up ahead looked like elk. He turned Flash back towards the barn. If it was a herd of elk, he didn't want to disturb them. So instead, he and

Flash traipsed back towards their other spot: the barn.

∞

"No worries, just get here when you can. You won't set me back." Ally held the phone to her ear as she continued curling Mrs. Randolph's hair in front of her. "Okay, see you in a few minutes, Ruby." She hung up and set her phone on her work counter, thankful for another appointment that emerged from her Hastings connection. Ruby Cole, Lawrence's fiancé, hadn't been able to make it back for a haircut that day a few weeks ago, so she needed a good trim to her pixie cut black hair. Ally was glad to do it. She'd wanted to get to know Ruby more after eating at her diner.

"I like that curling iron." Mrs. Randolph, a woman in her early forties who adored style, fashion, and cutting-edge beauty products, studied the brand name on the side.

Ally held it up. "It's one of my favorites. No matter what type of hair, it's an easy wand to use."

"I'll have to look at ordering one of those."

The bell above the salon door jingled and the room quieted a moment. Ally looked over and Lawrence Hastings along with his brother, Hayes, stood at the entrance. When Lawrence spotted her, he held his hands open in greeting. "Ally!" His boast caused all eyes to swing towards her. He tipped his hat to all the ladies he passed, Hayes following behind him at a leisurely pace. Lawrence draped his arm around her shoulders and gave her a good squeeze before nodding to the woman in the mirror. "Ma'am."

Mrs. Randolph actually blushed at his attention, and Ally couldn't hold back a small laugh as she turned to him. "What are you two doing here?"

"Look, Ruby may be callin' you about a haircut."

"She did."

"She coming?"

"On her way. Why?"

Lawrence fished in his wallet and grabbed a stack of cash and set it on the counter. "I want to pay for it, and while she's here I want you to give her the royal treatment."

"We only do haircuts, Lawrence."

"Oh." His face fell. "I thought you did nails and stuff."

Sandy walked forward and gently placed a hand on Lawrence's arm to draw his attention towards her. "Honey, what all did you want to do for her?"

"Spoil her." He removed his hat and held it in his hands, twirling it around in circles. "She never takes time to do anything for herself, so I thought while she's forced to sit still for five minutes, maybe I could treat her."

"Darlin'," Sandy held a hand to her heart. "you're a sweetheart." She grabbed the cash he left on Ally's counter and fished out the bills needed for a haircut and handed him the rest. "Why don't you go order her some flowers and have them sent here while she's here."

"That's an idea." He brightened and looked at Hayes, his brother quietly standing out of the way.

"How are you, Hayes?" Ally asked quietly as Lawrence and Sandy made special plans for Ruby.

He removed the hat on his head when she spoke his direction. "Oh, I'm good, Ally. How about you?"

"Good."

"And Ava?"

"Spunky, as usual."

He grinned at that. "Good to hear."

"You guys been busy spraying this week?" She lifted another strand of Mrs. Randolph's hair and wrapped it around the curling iron.

"Yes. That and I've been bucked way too many times by that unruly bronc I'm trying to break. We are headed to see Al over at the clinic." He pointed to his truck and trailer outside, the rambunctious horse pacing as much as he could inside the small space.

"Is something wrong with him?"

"Oh, he's got something going on with one of his ankles. And Al is on call tonight, so she wasn't going to be at the ranch later to check him out."

They paused a moment, both unsure what to say next, a slight awkwardness filling the air.

Mrs. Randolph held her hand out. "I'm Pamela."

Hayes smiled and shook her hand. "Hayes Hastings, nice to meet you, ma'am."

"Are you Ally's fella?" she asked. "I could tell something was different about her since the last time I came, but I couldn't put my finger on it."

Ally's face blanched in the mirror and her hands fumbled clumsily as she unwound the last curl.

Hayes's warm gaze washed over Ally before he looked at Mrs. Randolph. "No ma'am. Just a friend."

"Oh, poo," Pamela said and snapped her fingers. "Ally's the sweetest thing. I was hoping someone as handsome as you had come to sweep her off her feet."

Ally shook her head and smiled at her client. "How could I possibly win hearts around here when I have you to compete with?" She winked as her widowed client's cheeks tinged a small pink.

"Now you're just bein' silly." Pamela lightly patted her beautiful flowing curls as Ally removed the cloak from around her neck.

Pamela reached into her purse and began filling out a check for Ally. "You said your name was Hastings?"

"Yes ma'am."

"You part of the 7H Hastings?"

"Yes ma'am," Hayes said again.

"Ah." She paused in her writing and looked up. "I've heard about you. Are you the one marrying the woman at the vet clinic?"

"No ma'am. That'd be my brother Graham."

"I see. Well, I hear good things about your ranch. My late husband used to manage the Diamond X store here in town. Your ranch had an account with us."

"Was your husband Greg?" Hayes asked.

"That was him." A sad smile lifted her lips.

"Oh wow," Hayes sat in the free chair by Ally's workstation as Pamela continued to write. "He kept us clothed over the years. Didn't even have to go to the store, just had to call Greg, tell him what we needed, and he'd get it to us one way or another. I was sorry to hear about his passing."

"Thank you." She reached over and patted his hand, her eyes darting to Ally as she tidied up her counter. "Another person who goes above and beyond is this lady here." She looked up at Ally as she handed her the payment.

"I agree." Hayes winked at Ally. "If it weren't for Ally coming out to the ranch to cut hair, my brothers and I would look like cavemen."

Ally laughed. "Far from it, Hayes." She turned her attention back to her client. "Thanks, Pamela." Ally held her appointment book. "Three months for the next appointment?"

"Yes ma'am. Put me down. I'll need my ends seen to then. You take care until I see you again." She gave a small wave towards Hayes as she exited, and Lawrence walked up.

"Alright, we gotta get out of here. Ruby may be here any minute. I mapped out a plan with the lovely Sandy there." He motioned over his shoulder to Sandy talking into the phone. "Ready?"

Hayes stood and placed his hat on his head. "Yep."

Ally accepted the friendly hug from Lawrence. "Thanks, Ally."

"No problem."

Lawrence walked towards the door and Hayes lingered a moment. "Take care. Tell Ava I said hello." He placed his hat on his head and turned to leave.

Ally's hand jetted out and grabbed his arm, her heart racing at the feel of his skin beneath her fingers. He paused, his blue eyes settling upon her face. "I just wanted to let you know that I'm still open for lessons when you get the chance. I know we haven't spoken about them due to the spraying work, but I didn't want you to think I'd forgotten."

"I'm glad to hear that. I was hoping I hadn't put you off too long to where you just gave up on me."

"Not at all."

He placed his free hand on hers as it rested on his arm and he briefly brushed his thumb over the back of her hand. "Just let me know when. In fact—" He pointed towards her appointment book. "Got a free piece of paper in there?"

She quickly tore a page from the back of the book and handed it to him. He slipped a pen from his front shirt pocket and wrote his name and phone number down. "A little easier to contact me this way instead of chance encounters whenever my brothers have a romantic whim."

She chuckled at his remark and nodded. "I'll put you in my phone. Thanks."

"Shoot me a text so I can save your number. I'm pretty terrible about answering phone calls in the barn due to keeping it on silent so as not to disturb the horses. But a text will get my attention."

"I will."

His eyes roamed over her face once more and she felt the deep inhale fill her lungs at his intense perusal.

"Have a good day, Alejandra." He turned and followed his brother out towards his truck. As if the Hastings brothers were magnets polarized with women's eyes, every woman's gaze followed them through the windows. She felt her heart beat a bit faster when Hayes took one last look at the salon, as if knowing she still stared at him and gave a small wave before climbing into his truck. Her breath, which she hadn't realized she'd been holding, seeped out in one shaky breath as she watched disappointingly as he drove away.

Not ten minutes after the men left, Ruby buzzed into the salon. Having sat down and been draped in the cloak, her arrival was followed by flowers, fruit trays, champagne flutes, and chocolates for everyone in the building, courtesy of Lawrence. Gushing with love and excitement, Ruby and the rest of the ladies at Sandy's Salon indulged.

H

Chapter Nine

Though he was now open and free from spraying duties, Hayes waited for Ally's text or phone call saying she was ready for lessons. It never came. She hadn't even texted him so that he'd have her number in his phone. He tried not to let it bother him, but he'd thought there'd been a slight connection in the salon the week before when Lawrence doted on Ruby. Perhaps he was wrong. He was a bit rusty when it came to women. Maybe she'd changed her mind, despite her assurance.

"A penny for your thoughts?" Julia asked as she came to a halt atop Vivica's back next to him inside the pens. Her radiant smile instantly brightened his mood. At least he had one student making progress.

"You're a natural. And I think you're ready for the big reveal."

"Oh, I don't know about that." Julia dismounted and ran a soothing hand over Vivica's nose as she handed the reins to Hayes. "I was trying to think of some romantic way of asking Graham to come along on a ride, but I'm coming up empty."

"What about a picnic?"

Her eyes sparkled a moment and then her shoulders slumped. "When? He seems a bit busy lately."

Hayes rubbed his chin. "Tell you what, you just leave it to me. You be here tomorrow at lunch time, got it?"

"I work at the clinic tomorrow—" Julia started, but Hayes interrupted.

"So what? I'll talk to Al. And Ruby. I'll have Ruby prepare a basket for you. Or Annie. Whoever I can get a hold of. I'll have it ready for you here with Vivica at noon tomorrow. I'll tell Graham I need him to come look at Trisket for something, and he'll be here in two seconds flat."

"He'll be annoyed I'm pulling him away from his work."

"No, he won't. It's too hot to work from lunch until about four, so we've all been taking our afternoon siestas and working late instead. He'll have a few hours."

Julia pinched her lips as she contemplated his plan. "Tomorrow?"

"Tomorrow. You're ready, Jewels. Blow him away."

She grinned, lightly nibbling her lip in excitement at her surprise for Graham. "Okay. Tomorrow it is, then. You sure you don't mind organizing all of this?"

"Not at all. It's what brothers are for."

She reached forward and wrapped her arms around his neck and planted a kiss on his cheek. "And I'm thankful for you."

"Whoa, whoa, whoa, what is happening here?"

Lawrence's voice had them both turning their heads to find him leaning against his truck door, Alejandra and Ava riding in his passenger seats. All of them stared at Julia and Hayes.

"A simple thank you, dear Lawrence." Julia stepped back from Hayes and walked towards the other brother, looping her arm through his. "Mind giving me a ride back up to the house?"

"Do I get a kiss too?"

Julia laughed. "Sure."

HAYES

"Then consider it done." He wriggled his eyebrows and then motioned towards his passengers. "I have you some potential students, bro."

"I see that." Hayes walked towards the truck and opened the door, Ava hopping out immediately and wrapping a tight hug around his legs. He patted her back on a laugh as Ally stepped out of the truck. "What are you two ladies doing all the way out here?"

"It's a bit of a long story." Ally lightly swiped her hair from her eyes and looked at Vivica silently munching on grass. "I was at Annie's house cutting her hair, along with some of her church lady friends," Ally explained. "Lawrence came by and talk started about riding lessons, and I hadn't contacted you yet. Lawrence said you were giving lessons right now and he'd text you." She turned to see the brother's retreating truck. "I'm guessing he didn't, because you look surprised." Worry etched her smooth features at being uninvited.

"I just wrapped up Julia's lesson. Vivica is settled. I'm more than happy to get you two ladies in the saddle if that's what you'd like."

"You're sure? I know it is getting a bit late." Ally glanced at her watch and then shook her wrist. "I think it's broken. It still says it's three."

Hayes grinned. "Then it's not too late."

She fisted her hands on her hips. "Hayes," she continued, her tone telling him it wouldn't hurt her feelings if he didn't feel accommodating.

Ava looked up at the two of them. "So do I get to ride your horse, Mr. Hay?"

Hayes looked to Ally, and she finally relinquished a tired smile and nodded.

"Looks like you do, little lady. Follow me." He motioned towards Vivica. "Now, do you remember which side we saddle up on?"

She pointed and he nodded. "Good job." They walked around Vivica's head, Hayes giving the horse a friendly pat as he gripped her reins in his hand while also helping Ava into the saddle. "She ridin' by herself, Momma?" He looked to Ally.

"How do you feel, Mija?"

"I'm good." Ava flashed a thumbs up.

"Alright, then here we go. Hold onto the saddle horn there." Hayes began walking Vivica around the pens. Ally draped her arms over the fence, one foot resting on the bottom rung as she watched her daughter. "So, how was your day?" Hayes asked Ava.

"I had school," Ava reported, her tone reflecting her dislike of the topic. "Only for a little while though. Momma picked me up early to go do Ms. Annie's hair. I like Ms. Annie."

"Annie is pretty great."

"She likes you too. I asked her."

Hayes grinned at that as they made a small turn to head down the back of the pen. "I told her you were a prince like Mr. Gwaham. She thought that was funny and laughed."

"I bet she did."

"Ms. Annie said that you could only be a prince if you visited town more. Is that true?"

Hayes laughed. "Maybe so, but I also know that's just Annie's way of inviting me over for supper sometime. She gets to missin' us out here."

"I told her you went to town to see Momma at Ms. Sandy's salon, so that meant you were a prince."

"How did you know I went to Ms. Sandy's?" He looked up at her and she flushed, her eyes darting towards her mother. "I heard Momma talking to Lita about it on her phone. Don't tell her. She'll be mad at me for hearing."

"I won't say a word." Hayes looked up and ran his fingers over his lips like a zipper. "But you know it's not nice to listen in on other people's conversations."

"I know. I try not to, but I like hearing Momma laugh, and she always laughs with Lita."

Hayes' heart twinged a bit at that statement. Alejandra laughing must be a rare thing to capture. Who was he to scold Ava on cherishing that moment? "That's a good reason."

"Momma said she likes you and your family. Said Ms. Julia would be a nice friend to have."

"She's right on that," Hayes agreed. "Julia is a rare gem."

"Do you love her?" Ava asked.

Surprised at the gumption of such a small person, Hayes looked up to see her dark little gaze staring straight at him. "In a way," he began. "She's going to be my new sister, so of course I love her like she is a part of my family."

"But Mr. Gwaham has her heart?" Ava asked.

"Yes. He does."

"I heard Momma talkin' about that with Lita. Momma's never had someone get her heart." Ava sighed, rubbing a gentle hand between Vivica's ears as they walked. "Have you ever had someone get your heart, Mr. Hay?"

"You mean besides you?" He winked up at her as she grinned. "I haven't."

Silence stretched as they walked over towards Ally and she softly clapped her hands to cheer Ava on as they came to a halt. "She's becoming an expert." Hayes tipped his hat towards Ava as he helped her out of the saddle. She climbed over the fence and watched as her mother did the same, only to the other side where Hayes stood. "You up for riding by yourself? Or do you want me to ride with you?"

"I think I will try by myself today."

"Alright." Hayes waved his hand towards the stirrup and Ally hoisted herself onto the horse's back. He looked at Ava. "You stay right there at the fence."

"Yes sir." Ava climbed to sit on the railing and Hayes began leading Ally around the pens. "So how was your time at Annie's?"

"Oh, it was great. I got to hear all the town gossip, learn more about you and your brothers, and be set up with two grandsons."

He laughed. "That's all?"

"Annie told me you sing," Ally prodded. "And really well from what the other ladies said too."

He looked up at her and shrugged his shoulders. "Just at church and around the house."

"I think Ms. Betty said it was the voice of an angel."

He snorted before laughing. "Betty would say that. She's been after me to join the church choir for years."

"Why don't you?"

Wanting to give an honest answer that didn't require too much of a dive into his personal life, Hayes took a deep inhale. "My mother could sing. What little memories I have of her, she was always singin'." He smiled up at her. "She was in the church choir. My daddy would cry when she'd sing her solos. There was something special in that." He paused. "I just don't know if I could get up there and sing and not think about that."

"That's special." Ally's voice softened.

"So, I just sing around the house, the ranch, and in the pew. I enjoy it though. My horses," he grimaced. "not so much."

She grinned as she glanced over at the fence. "Ava." Her voice caught and his eyes darted to the fence to see Ava had disappeared. He hurried his steps towards the gate, tying off Vivica. He left Ally in the saddle as he sprinted towards the barn. Ally had successfully dismounted on her own and was hot on his heels. He barged inside, his eyes adjusting in time to see Ava reaching a hand towards the latch on the stall that housed the rowdy bronc he'd been attempting to break. "Ava, no!" he barked, his voice stern and loud as he sprinted forward as the latch gave way. The horse's hooves slammed against the stall door and it ricocheted off the back wall, barely missing Ava. Her eyes wide, Ava watched as the horse barreled out of the stall and towards Hayes and Ally, not even noticing the small girl standing nearest to him. The horse rampaged towards Ally and Hayes dived in time to knock her out of its way as it slammed through the barn doors and hit open pasture. They landed with a thud in hay and dirt, and Ally's heartbeat matched the panicked rhythm of his own as her fingers gripped his biceps. He looked up to see a stunned Ava standing on the other side of the barn. Before he could speak, Ally gripped his shoulders, rolled him over to his back to free herself from underneath him, and began to stand, her deep brown eyes livid as she stared at her daughter.

∞

"Ava Marie!" Ally barked, stomping towards her daughter. "You know you are to *never* come into this barn alone. You know that Mr. Hayes is the *only* one to handle the horses. Podrías haberte matado. No siguió las reglas. No volveremos a montar a caballo." She paused when she noticed her daughter's eyes widen and realized she'd slipped into Spanish. She placed a calming hand to her forehead. "Get out of the barn now." She pointed, and Ava slowly walked towards them, giving Ally a wide berth. She followed after her and began scolding Ava further about disappearing and putting them all in danger. She didn't like to see her daughter cry, but the fear that coursed through Ally's veins at seeing her small hand reach for that latch still had her adrenaline pumping. Hayes exited the barn, tapping his now dirty hat against his pant leg. Ava sneaked a sniffly glance his direction, swiping her arm over her nose. "You need to tell Mr. Hayes you are sorry for disobeying."

Ava took two steps towards Hayes and froze, her hands flying up over her eyes as she began to wail. Ally's shoulders and head dropped as she inwardly berated herself for being a terrible mother, guest at the ranch, and anything else she could think of.

Hayes walked towards Ava and knelt in front of her. He gently tugged her daughter's hands down and gave them a brief squeeze before scooping her up into his arms for a tight hug. He gently brushed Ava's hair out of her eyes, and tucked the strands sticking in her tears behind her ears. He lifted her onto his side and walked towards Ally. "How about we all take a walk?"

"Hayes—" Ally didn't even know what to say, but she accepted the free hand he extended to her. She recognized the path behind the barn that led to his house and allowed herself the luxury of indulging in his hand hold. His palms were rough, but his touch gentle, and she just hadn't gotten to hold a man's hand in quite some time. It felt nice. It felt easy... with Hayes. Ava continued to cry, but her wails had softened to whimpers and sniffles in Hayes' shirt collar as they approached his house. Yegua ran out to greet them as they walked through his front gate and up the stone path towards his porch. He released Ally's hand to open the front door and ushered her inside ahead of himself. He then closed the door and walked Ava towards a small dining table nestled to the side of the kitchen and eased her into a chair. "Have a seat." He pointed to another free chair, and Ally felt herself slide into it as if all her energy and adrenaline had been sucked out of her. He walked to the refrigerator and grabbed two beers, handing one to Ally and taking the other for himself. He popped the top and took one long sip before setting it on the counter. He washed his hands and then began removing ingredients from his pantry and refrigerator. He poured a small glass of milk and added some powdered cacao mix, stirring it up and handing it Ava. She watched him through glassy eyes, just as confused as her mother.

He mixed and added ingredients to a large bowl until satisfied, draping a dish towel over the top of it. He then reached for a bag of goldfish crackers and walked them towards the table, pouring some on a napkin for Ava. He then sat in one of the remaining two chairs and looked at Ally. He reached over and squeezed her hand before turning towards Ava. "How you doin', butter bean?"

Her little hand hesitated over a cracker as her dark eyes began to brim with tears again. Hayes nodded as if he understood. "You know why your momma's upset, right?"

She nodded.

"You know I have rules for my barn," Hayes continued, and she nodded again. "Why did you go into the barn?"

Ava inhaled a shaky breath, her eyes darting between the two adults before she finally confessed. "I heard the horse wanting to get out."

"And you went to help him?"

She nodded. "He seemed scared in there." She dropped her eyes to her hands in her lap, her bottom lip in a permanent pout. Ally watched as Hayes gently rested a hand on the back of her daughter's chair. "That was sweet of you to want to help him, Ava." Her daughter looked up at him. "But the rules of the barn are to listen to me, right?"

"Yes." Her voice was barely above a whisper.

"And you're not allowed to wander around without me."

"Yes sir."

"How did you feel when the horse ran out of his stall towards your momma?"

"Scared," she whispered, darting her eyes towards Ally.

"We were scared too," he admitted. "We could have been hurt."

"But you rescued her," Ava added.

"I'm glad I was able to. But you see why we have rules in the barn? If we let a horse out, especially one that isn't trained, it could be a dangerous situation. Someone could get hurt." He pointed to Ally's arm and she realized she had a small gash on her elbow.

"I'm sorry, Momma," Ava said. "And I'm sorry for not listenin', Mr. Hay."

"Well, I forgive you. And I bet, if you give your momma a big hug, she'll forgive you too, if she hasn't already." He looked up and winked at Ally and her breath caught at the compassion in his blue eyes. Ava slid out of her chair and hurled herself into Ally's arms, Ally rubbing a hand down her daughter's silky hair. She mouthed a 'thank you' towards Hayes and he nodded, standing to his feet. He clapped his hands, bringing Ava's eyes back to him. "Now that we have gone over the rules again, how about we eat some supper? You hungry?"

Ava eyed him curiously as he walked back into the kitchen, glancing over at the table in mock surprise that she didn't follow. "Now, how am I to make a pizza without help?" Ava's lips trembled into a rejuvenated smile as she looked up at Ally for permission.

"Go on." She released her hold on Ava and watched as Hayes moved a chair to the counter for her to stand in.

He placed a cheese grater in front of her daughter. "Know how to use one of these?"

Ava nodded enthusiastically as he handed her a block of cheese. "You get started on that while I take your momma to the bathroom to clean her cut, okay?"

"Yes sir."

"She okay in the chair?" he asked Ally.

She gave a nod as he tilted his head towards the hallway and a small half bath. He fished underneath the cabinet and grabbed a small first aid kit. "Thank you," she said again. "For being so kind to her after what happened. I am so sorry she released your horse." Gasping, Ally gripped his arms. "Oh, Hayes, your horse! He's still out there. Do we need to catch him?"

He shook his head. "He can't go far. Besides, he needs to run off some of his temper."

"But what about predators? Coyotes?"

"He'll be fine." Hayes gently grabbed her arm and began dabbing her elbow with a cotton ball drenched in hydrogen peroxide. The sting was brief due to the tingles from Hayes' touch. He was gentle in dealing with Ava when he had every right to scream and kick them out. He'd risked his own life to push her out of the way of the horse's charge, and now he tenderly cleansed her wounds as if unaffected by the day's events. He looked up and startled at her watching him so closely.

"I apologize if I overstepped," Hayes mumbled.

"You didn't. You had every right to... well, to scold her. You were calmer than I would have been. I am just... so sorry for what happened."

"She has a tender heart. I didn't want to punish that aspect. But if she is to come for lessons, she has to obey the rules. And I have to be able to trust her to do that."

"I understand. I'll be talking with her some more about it. Are you still willing to teach her?"

"Sure, I am." The corner of his mouth tipped up into a small smirk. "Today was a lesson learned type of day. Sometimes we need those. Just ask Clint." He chuckled as he placed a band aid on her elbow and held it up for inspection. "As good as new." He placed a quick kiss on the injury and then paused as if realizing his actions. He cleared his throat and took a step away from her, releasing his hold on her arm. "She's probably pretty close to being done with the cheese." He motioned over his shoulder and started to walk back towards the kitchen, but Ally grabbed his hand. He paused as she threaded her fingers through his and gently tugged him towards her. His steps were slow and measured as he crowded her space, and Ally felt her heart erupt in her chest at his nearness. She rested her forehead against his as she breathed in the scent of him: hay, horses, and sunshine. He didn't pressure her into a kiss, he didn't do anything but wait, patient as he always was, and her stomach fluttered. His finger lightly brushed from her shoulder down to her hand, sending a heat wave in its path. Their noses bumped slightly, and she heard his small intake of breath that made her wish to melt into his arms even further.

"Mr. Hay! I'm done!" Ava's voice called from the kitchen.

"Should we go check on her?" he asked quietly, his voice hoarse as his fingers gently played with the tips of her long braid.

"Yes." Ally's hushed reply brought her a breath closer to him and she gently pressed her lips to his, allowing the hand on her braid to gently slide behind her neck as he held her to him. He glided his lips over hers, testing, as if trying to be as delicate as possible. Trembling, Ally gently tugged away, her eyes focused on his nervous smile. "I... um..." She tugged away from his touch completely and stepped towards the kitchen. Ava's soft voice singing a song about kittens drifted to them. Hayes followed behind her, his presence an electric heat that seemed to shoot bolts of warmth and excitement through her as she watched her daughter toss the pizza dough from the bowl into the air and catch it. Hayes' deep chuckle had her giving him another apologetic look as the mess of her daughter's enthusiasm tarnished his clean kitchen.

He gently tapped Ally's elbow as he passed her and stepped to Ava's side. "Lookin' good, butter bean. Are you a professional pizza maker?"

Her daughter's giggles and Hayes' electric gaze had her face splitting into a wide smile as she walked towards them to soak in the small moment of joy and togetherness.

H

Chapter Ten

"Did you lose something?" Clint held the reins of the bronc that had escaped the barn the previous day due to Ava's help. Hayes nodded his thanks.

"Where'd you find him?"

"In the garden, of all places. Annie's going to have a fit when she sees what he did to some of her plants."

"We'll blame Seth." Hayes smirked as he took the reins from his brother and led the horse back to its stall.

"How'd he get out, anyway?" Clint asked.

"There was a mishap here at the barn."

"A mishap?" Clint asked, his brows disappearing under his cowboy hat. "Those don't happen here."

"Well, Ally and Ava were here for riding lessons yesterday and Ava let him out."

Clint's jaw tightened. "That wasn't a great idea."

"No. It wasn't."

"You allowing her to come back?"

"Yes."

Clint crossed his arms and leaned against one of the wooden support posts as he watched Hayes give the bronc a brush down. "That's not like you. If I broke a Hayes Rule, would I get to come back? Because I recall I once forgot to latch the gate and I wasn't allowed back at the pens for a few weeks."

"That was different."

"How so?"

Hayes looked at his younger brother. "You wouldn't understand."

"Try me."

Hayes stared at Clint a moment longer. "I like her."

"The kid?"

"Well, yeah, but I meant that I like Ally."

"As in you have feelings for her?"

"I think I might."

"So that's why the kid gets a free pass?"

"She doesn't get a free pass." Hayes' hackles rose. "We talked it out. She understood what she did was wrong because she almost hurt her momma in the process. But that's not the point."

"So, you like the pretty hairdresser." Clint waved his hand for Hayes to continue.

"Yeah. I do."

"She has a kid."

"I'm aware of that."

"You prepared to date someone who has a kid?"

Hayes exited the stable and then motioned towards the tack room so he could sort through the feed. Out of curiosity, he asked, "Have you ever dated a woman with a kid?"

Clint helped lift a bag of cubes and tossed it towards the pile in the corner. "Once."

"And how was it? I mean, was it hard to work around an extra person?"

"Not really."

"Then why didn't it work out?"

"The kid was a brat," Clint explained. "I just didn't have the tolerance."

"Oh." Hayes shook his head. "Ava's not a brat. She's a great kid. A bit spirited, but I think that's a good thing."

"And her momma?" Clint asked.

"Beautiful." Hayes' lips tilted a bit as he took a minute to think about Ally. "She has the darkest eyes, and her hair feels like silk. And she has this habit of slipping in and out of Spanish when she gets worked up that just—" He held a hand over his heart and widened his eyes as if he were about to faint.

Clint bit back a laugh as he nodded. "Yep, you've got the feelings. Let me just pull out the Hastings chart and scratch your name off now."

"I wouldn't go that far yet. I think I've got my work cut out for me to convince Ally I'm good enough."

Offended for his brother, Clint straightened. "Why on earth would she not think you're good enough? You're a Hastings. And beyond that, you're Hayes Hastings. You're the nicest one of us. You've had a steady head on your shoulders since we were kids. And you've always been nice. Too nice sometimes, but nice. If she's got a problem with y—"

Hayes held up his hand to stop his brother's rant, and then patted Clint's shoulder in thanks before he continued. "Thanks for that. I don't think it has anything to do with me, per se. I think she has a nervousness when it comes to men in general. She doesn't trust us. And from what it seems like she's been through, I don't blame her. Seems she had it rough with Ava's dad. I don't know the full story, but I understand why she'd be cautious. But then yesterday, when she kissed me, it just felt... nice. Like, real nice."

"She kissed you?" Clint smiled. "What's with all these women kissing my brothers? I've never had a date who kissed me first."

"Really?" Hayes asked. "That's surprising... since you've had so many," he teased.

Clint harumphed and waited for Hayes to keep talking.

"Guess you better step it up with Kara," Hayes suggested.

"Kara is off the list."

"What? Why? I thought you liked her?"

"I did and do. But rumor has it, aka Ruby told me, that Kara and Jimmy, the vet tech, have been dating the last few weeks. And I'm about to leave for New Mexico. So, I leave as a free bird." He held his hands out to his sides presenting himself as he was. "We'll see how the New Mexico women like me." He winked, causing Hayes to laugh.

"Look out, New Mexico."

"But this isn't about me and my stately charm." Clint followed Hayes outside and into the dimmed sun as the clouds promised the potential of rain. "This is about you navigating a woman, a single mom with trust issues, and a kid. What's your plan?"

"I don't really have one." Hayes rubbed a tired hand over the back of his neck. "I'm just going to be patient. I figure that's all I can do. Let things progress at their own speed. I like Ally. I'd like to… see her more? Date her? Court her? What's really the term to use these days?"

Clint laughed. "How about 'all of the above'?"

"Yeah. All of that, then. But I don't want to pressure her. I think she is trying to make it on her own with Ava. I don't want her to feel like I'm threatening that."

"But how are you to have a relationship if she just wants to be alone?"

"That's the dilemma."

"Has she told you she wants to be alone?"

"Not exactly. We haven't talked since yesterday. I'm not sure where she stands at this point. I know she doesn't want to complicate things— her work for Julia, and that type of thing."

"Women." Clint shook his head. "I don't get it. They want a good man, but then when one comes along, they act like they don't want one."

"That's just it... Ally has never said she wants a relationship. She may not even want a man, period. She may want to take on the world with just her and Ava. It's not about her not wanting me because I'm a good guy, the hurdle is her even wanting a relationship, period. How do I convince her she does?"

"And with you?"

"Well, yeah, that's ultimately my goal," Hayes admitted. "I mean, Ava would thrive on this ranch. Ally could still cut hair in town or in Sheffield if she wanted. I wouldn't hinder her professional goals. I'd support whatever she'd like to do."

"Wait, you just jumped from courting to having them on the ranch."

"Yeah. So?"

"That's a big leap. That's more than a little interest, brother. That's you saying you want to marry her one day, if you want her here on the ranch."

"I—" Hayes paused, not realizing that is what he'd meant, and surprised that his heart was thinking along those lines already. "I guess I am thinking about that, eventually."

Clint exhaled a deep breath and shook his head. "Yep. You're a goner. Good luck with that."

"Gee, thanks." Hayes shrugged on a sigh. "I guess we'll see how it goes.

"I don't have any advice. I haven't met that person that makes me think long term yet. You'd be better off talkin' to Cal or Lawrence. I'd suggest Graham too, but I think he's still as baffled as the rest of us as to how he won Julia over, so I'd focus on the other two."

Hayes chuckled. "Maybe I will. Thanks for bringing Tick back."

"Tick? You're naming the horse Tick?"

"For now."

"Why?"

"Because he ticks me off."

Clint grinned. "Fitting." He walked back towards his truck, Hayes just realizing that his brother wore a pressed shirt and his nicest pair of boots.

"Where are you headed?"

"Oh, I have a date." Clint's smile held a touch of mischief.

"I can't keep up with you. And I have no idea how you do it."

"It's a gift. Later, brother." He tossed a wave out his driver-side window as he drove towards the main hub of the ranch to head to town.

8

"Thanks for coming on such short notice." Julia motioned for Ally to come inside the guest house. She smiled down at Ava following behind her mother, and then an older woman as well.

"This is my mother," Ally introduced. "She was with us when you called. I hope you don't mind."

"Not at all. Welcome." She shook the woman's hand. "I'm Julia."

"Ah, bonita."

Julia's smiled widened. "Thank you. Come on in. I know it seems frivolous to go to so much trouble getting my makeup done today, but I want this moment to be special. I'm to meet Graham in an hour. Is that enough time?"

"Yes. More than enough." Ally smiled. "We'll do a different, lighter look for you today so we can save the wedding look for the special day."

"Perfect. I have some sweet tea on the island there. Please help yourself. I'm sorry, I didn't get your name." Julia looked to Ally's mom.

"Lita."

"Everyone just calls her Lita, instead of her real name, which is Marie."

"Lita it is, then." Julia waved towards the drinks. "Where do you want me?" Julia asked.

"Let's sit by the front window. There's great natural light right here."

"Okay, perfect."

Ally settled across from Julia and they quickly began applying primer to her face. "So how was your time with Hayes yesterday?"

Ally paused a moment before continuing to spread the serum over Julia's smooth skin. "It was good."

"We made pizza," Ava stated as she plopped onto the couch next to her grandmother.

"You did? That sounds yummy."

"It was. Mr. Hay was super nice to me, even after I broke his rules."

Julia wondered what that meant, but didn't press the issue, for which Ally was thankful.

"He rescued Momma from the wild horse. He was her prince."

Lita's eyes sparkled at that information; new information, which Ally had not told her mother when she'd arrived in town early that morning.

"Is this Hayes your brother?" Lita asked Julia.

"Future brother-in-law," Julia explained.

"I want to meet this Hayes. To thank him, of course." She smiled at her daughter's sudden clumsiness at the mention of the man's name.

"That could definitely happen. I'm headed straight over to him after this." Julia closed her eyes as Ally applied eyeshadow to her eye lids. "I'm planning a romantic horse ride and picnic with Graham, and Hayes has been helping me pull it off."

"A romantic man, hm?"

"He's a sweetheart," Julia confirmed. "And he'd do anything for anyone."

"And he rescued you, Mija?" Lita asked.

"He did," Ally confirmed. "A horse was released from its stall and charged towards me. Hayes... pushed me out of the way."

"They fell and got real dirty," Ava added. "But then Mr. Hay took us home and we made pizza."

"And you like Mr. Hayes?" Lita asked Ava.

The little girl nodded emphatically. "He's a prince like Mr. Gwaham. And Momma's going to be his princess."

Ally flushed. "Ava Marie, that is not true. Do not say things that are not true."

"Why not, Momma? Mr. Hay is nice."

"He is. He's very nice." Ally's voice softened at her daughter's hopeful eyes. "But..."

Julia eyed Ally closely. "He's a great man," she whispered. "Should you ever consider dating someone, he'd be a great choice. And that's all I will say so I do not overstep and scare you away."

Ally held Julia's understanding gaze a moment before looking down at the makeup compact in her hand and swiping a fluffy brush through pink blush for Julia's cheeks.

"I am determined to make a life for me and my daughter. On my own terms."

"Ella es obstinada." Lita frowned briefly before patting Ava's leg and taking a sip of her tea.

"There's nothing wrong with being stubborn," Ally defended. "I wasted too much time on... well, you know who. I will not do that again."

"Not all men are the same, Mija," Lita continued.

"And that is all we are going to say with little ears present," Ally scolded her mother, and Lita and Julia shared a brief knowing look.

"Well, you are welcome to come see the stables, Lita, when I head that way," Julia invited. "Hayes keeps the barn, pens, and horses beautiful. It's quite a sight."

"I would love to, Julia."

And that's just what they did. Mostly because Ally's mother wouldn't let the matter drop. She was determined to meet Hayes. And Ally had to admit, despite her fluttering heart and nerves, she wanted to see him again too. She just hadn't spoken to him after their kiss the previous evening, and she wasn't sure how to act around him. Had it meant something? She had been the one to initiate it. And though she talked of not needing or wanting a man in her life, the thought of it being Hayes didn't scare her so much. When they pulled up to the stables, Hayes stood with Trisket and Vivica, both horses looking freshly brushed and saddled. He walked back into the barn, oblivious to the arriving vehicle and the women stepped out. Lita inhaled a deep breath of fresh air. "Es—"

"Breathtaking," Ally finished for her and Lita nodded with a whimsical smile.

Hayes walked out of the barn, a square bale of hay within the grip of his gloved hands as he walked towards the pens. He stopped in his tracks when he saw the women. "Oh. Afternoon." He smiled as he finished his task.

"Oh, Mija..." Lita trailed off in appreciation of the handsome cowboy.

"Shhh," Ally warned and lightly tapped Ava's shoulder to start walking.

Hayes removed his gloves as Julia walked up in appreciation at the basket strapped to Vivica's saddle. "This looks wonderful, Hayes."

"Annie whipped together something pretty tasty. I'd say I was jealous, but she made me my own basket too."

"I'm sure it will be amazing."

"You want to already be in the saddle when he drives up? Or wait?"

"I'd like to be in the saddle, maybe I could round the corner or something?"

"A little dramatic entrance. I like it." He grinned at his future sister-in-law and nodded in agreement. "I'll text him now, and that will give us about five minutes until he whips in here in a frenzy."

"Alright." Julia flashed a nervous smile towards the women and Ally gave her an encouraging thumbs up.

Hayes grabbed Vivica's reins as Julia climbed into the saddle and he walked her behind the barn to wait. He then texted his older brother.

He pocketed his phone and looked up at his extra company. "And good afternoon to you ladies. What brings you out here?"

Ava ran forward and hugged his legs and he chuckled.

"Well, now, that's a good enough reason. How are you, butter bean?"

"Good." Ava looked adoringly up at him, and Ally's heart skipped a beat further when he gently brushed his hand over her daughter's hair.

"Are you going to introduce me to this beautiful lady?" He motioned towards her grandmother and Ava bounced towards Lita.

"This is my Lita."

Hayes removed his cowboy hat with one hand and extended the other. "Nice to meet you, ma'am. I'm Hayes Hastings."

Lita shook his hand with a firm grip and a pleased smile.

"My mother came into town this morning and then Julia called."

"Ah. It's a big day for her. And if you'll excuse me for just a minute—" He pointed to Graham's truck rushing towards the stables, his brother in fear that something was wrong with his horse.

"Where do we need to go to not be in the way?" Ally asked.

"You're fine where you're at." Hayes lightly squeezed her elbow as he walked past her to intercept his brother.

Graham hopped out of his truck, his long and purposeful strides speaking volumes to his panic. His eyes fluttered over the unexpected guests and he tampered down his panic. "What's the matter?" He walked towards Trisket, already running his hands over his horse seeking out injury.

"Well, about that—" Hayes rubbed a nervous hand over the back of his neck, hoping that Julia's wonderful surprise would prevent him receiving a punch to the gut for fooling his older brother. He nodded over his shoulder as Julia and Vivica rounded the back of the barn.

Graham's gaze darted up and back to Hayes and then back up towards Julia. She beamed, looking the part of gushing bride-to-be as her eyes fell upon Graham. "Wha— How— Is this—" He didn't know what to say as his shoulders relaxed and Julia reached a hand towards him. He kissed her palm without a thought.

"I plan to whisk you away for a picnic, Mr. Hastings." Julia pointed at the basket on the back of Vivica. "Will you join me?"

Graham's eyes never left her as he watched her expertly navigate Vivica towards the gate.

"Trisket is fine, by the way," Hayes whispered, handing his brother the reins. "Let's just hope she can keep up." He winked at Graham as his older brother, dumbfounded, climbed into his saddle and followed quietly after his fiancé. Hayes smiled as he watched them go, Graham continually staring in disbelief at Julia as they went.

"And just like that, she just made him fall even more in love with her," Hayes announced on a laugh. "Now, I'm assuming you ladies didn't come for a riding lesson, so how about some lunch?"

"Oh, we didn't intend to interfere with your day," Ally began. "My mom wanted to see the stables and Julia invited her to come see."

"I'm glad she did." Hayes nodded towards Lita. "How was your trip from El Paso?" He walked towards her mother and let her drape her arm over his elbow as he escorted her towards the barn to show her the horses, her mother chatting his ear off.

Ava looked up at Ally's face. "Mr. Hay is real nice, Momma."

"I know, sweetie."

"I want him to be your prince."

"There's more to it than that, Ava."

Her daughter shrugged. "I'm going too." She followed after Hayes, grabbing his free hand as they entered the barn.

His acceptance was natural, and his stride never wavered as he led the two in the barn. He glanced over his shoulder. "You coming?"

She nodded silently, his blue eyes wary a moment before she took the first step his direction. His face lifted into a handsome smile as he leaned down to hear what her mother was saying.

When she'd reached the barn, her mother and Ava were feeding his horse, Flash, some carrots and Hayes waited to the side of the door for her. "I wanted to call you."

She jumped at his voice and placed a hand over her heart.

"Sorry, didn't mean to scare you." He reached for her hand and she took a step away, his hand hovering in the air. He took her signal and dropped it back to his side, disappointment written on his features.

"I also wanted to talk to you," Ally began. "Yesterday was... well, it can't happen again."

His face fell even further into a scowl, if Hayes' face could even hold such an expression. He redirected his gaze towards Ava and Lita, always watchful inside the barn.

"I don't mean to be mean, Hayes," Ally whispered. "I just... there's a lot you don't know about me. And I've worked hard to be where I'm at. Ava and I have been through some hard times. I don't want her to experience anymore of that."

"And you think I would cause her harm?"

"No. Not intentionally," Ally added. "She's already attached to you. I think it's best it is as a friend instead of with wishful thoughts of you being my prince. She already wants that, and you rescuing me yesterday didn't help matters there."

"I'd never hurt her. Or you." His voice was firm, his eyes taking a sudden hardness that she'd never seen before. Offense at her insinuation that he would.

"I know you wouldn't mean to. But—"

"No buts." He slashed his hand through the air. "I wouldn't. Ever. It's not who I am. I thought after yesterday, after our—" He motioned between the two of them. "Well, after the kiss, that you saw that. I'm trustworthy, Ally. I believe in honor and integrity. I believe in saying and doing what you mean. If the kiss meant nothing to you, then yeah, it doesn't need to happen again. Because all it did was make me want things I didn't realize I wanted. I was content with my life here on the ranch. Solo. Alone. Then you and Ava come into my life and give me a small glimpse at what it could be to share my life with someone else. I'd like that with you. I know that now. But if it's not on the table, then I'm sorry, I can't. I can't give you lessons anymore. It wouldn't be fair for me to feel like this and only have you at arm's length. I hope you understand."

"We still have so much we don't know about each other," Ally stated.

"And? That's what dating is for, right? We get to know one another better."

"Dating is hard when I have a daughter in the mix."

"It's only hard if you make it hard." Hayes placed his hands on his hips. "But I'm tough. I can handle it. I like Ava. I don't see her as a hurdle or obstruction in getting to know you. I see her as a blessing."

Ally's heart squeezed at that and she studied him a moment, seeing the truth of his statement in his eyes.

"Give me a shot, Ally. I'm not looking to rescue you. You're more than capable of doing that yourself, which is evident, because you have. What I'm asking is if you'll rescue me."

Her breath caught as he took a step towards her, his hands reaching for hers, only this time she didn't pull away.

"Thanks to you and Ava, I don't want to be alone out here anymore. I didn't realize I needed someone special in my life until you two ladies came along. But last night showed me how empty my life has been. Please, just give me a chance." Hayes waited, patiently, as he always did.

Ally glanced over towards her mother and caught her eye. Lita gave a small nod of approval as she flicked her gaze to their joined hands. Ally turned back to Hayes. "I'm scared, Hayes. Nervous."

"Me too." He brushed his thumbs over her knuckles. "And that is new for me. But maybe we could be scared together. Maybe that's how it is supposed to be. We'll be stronger together."

"It will take time for me to fully—"

"I'm a patient man. I can wait as long as necessary if the end goal is having you and Ava in my life." She leaned her forehead against his. He tenderly brushed a hand down her long braid, his fingers fiddling with the end before he slightly gave it a playful tug. "Give me a chance, Ally."

She felt his hands slide to her hips and his lips a whisper from her own as he waited for her response. Feeling the flush of emotion rising from her heart she whispered, "Está bien, mi vaquero," and sealed their fresh beginning with a kiss.

∞

Five Months Later

A February burn meant by spring the pastures would be full of lush grass in time for Graham and Julia's wedding. The conditions were perfect. A nice fifty degrees, twenty percent humidity, and the wind was at a snail's pace below ten miles per hour. They couldn't pass the opportunity. They'd been waiting for that southeast wind so the fire wouldn't burn towards the highway. It was now or never. Calvin had taken care of maintaining the fire breaks around December so all that was needed were the perfect conditions and a ready crew. They'd touched up Calvin's work the last couple of days in preparation, they'd mapped the ten-day forecast like a hunt for buried treasure, and they'd readied all the equipment, water trucks, tanks, and utility vehicles that would be needed. Pocket radios had been charged and at the ready. And as they stood around Graham's truck for one final game plan talk. The brothers, including Clint, who'd returned from New Mexico, listened carefully.

The wind was supposed to pick up after lunch and so their window of time needed to be used strategically. Graham whipped out a notepad and began drawing out a map of the burn area.

"This is the burn block. We are here by the red gate. Wind is coming out of the west, so we are going to go to the east side which is over there," He pointed. "and we're going to light from the southeast corner to the northeast corner with a backfire."

Graham looked up at Clint and Seth. "You two are the spotters to make sure no fire jumps the lines." The brothers nodded in obedience.

"Hayes and I will light the fire. Cal, you'll be in the tractor, Philip and Lawrence, you two will be in the water trucks. Everyone keep your positions. If the flames get too hot, we'll back off. Keep your radios handy." A truck pulled up and Alice, driving, and Julia, Ally, Ava, Helena, and Ruby all in the bed of the truck watched them.

"Did someone call reinforcements?" Hayes asked, his smile mirrored on all the other brothers' faces as they saw their special lady.

"Julia still doesn't understand the purpose of burning," Graham muttered. "She thinks I'm ruining our wedding spot."

"She'll understand... in a couple of months," Cal teased.

"Don't get distracted," Graham barked, his face hard as he studied the pasture and the weather conditions.

He noticed Philip, Calvin, Lawrence, and Hayes looking towards the women. "Fine," Graham barked. "Go give them all a kiss and then we get started."

Hayes didn't have to be told twice. He darted over to the truck and high-fived Ava as he hopped on the tire and hoisted himself up to eye level with Ally. Without a word, he pressed his lips firmly against hers. Her fingers brushed his jaw, and he pulled away, eyes dancing. "Come to watch me set the world on fire?"

Ally laughed. "I think you've done that already. For me, anyway." She kissed him again and Ava draped her arms around his neck for a hug before he hopped down. He tapped Lawrence's back with a slap as his brother wasn't quite ready to leave Ruby behind. She hopped out, deciding to ride with him in the water truck.

"Alright, let's go," Graham called, giving Julia's hand a reassuring squeeze to trust him. The men then took their positions.

"Come on, girls." Alice cranked the engine of Cal's work truck. "Let's watch our flames set flames."

Hayes glanced over at the truck one more time, Ally holding up her hand in a small wave, her nervous eyes watching him closely. He tipped his hat her direction, thankful, grateful, and blessed.

Continue the story with

Order Here:
https://www.amazon.com/dp/B091Z917SN

THE SIBLINGS O'RIFCAN SERIES   KATHARINE E. HAMILTON

The Complete Siblings O'Rifcan Series Available in Paperback, Ebook, and Audiobook

Claron

https://www.amazon.com/dp/B07FYR44KX

Riley

https://www.amazon.com/dp/B07G2RBD8D

Layla

https://www.amazon.com/dp/B07HJRL67M

Chloe

https://www.amazon.com/dp/B07KB3HG6B

Murphy

https://www.amazon.com/dp/B07N4FCY8V

All titles in The Lighthearted Collection Available in Paperback, Ebook, and Audiobook

Chicago's Best
https://www.amazon.com/dp/B06XH7Y3MF

Montgomery House
https://www.amazon.com/dp/B073T1SVCN

Beautiful Fury
https://www.amazon.com/dp/B07B527N57

McCarthy Road
https://www.amazon.com/dp/B08NF5HYJG

Check out the Epic Fantasy Adventure Available in Paperback, Ebook, and Audiobook

THE UNFADING LANDS

The Unfading Lands

https://www.amazon.com/dp/B00VKWKPES

Darkness Divided, Part Two in The Unfading Lands Series

https://www.amazon.com/dp/B015QFTAXG

Redemption Rising, Part Three in The Unfading Lands Series

https://www.amazon.com/dp/B01G5NYSEO

Subscribe to Katharine's Newsletter for news on upcoming releases and events!
https://www.katharinehamilton.com/subscribe.html

Find out more about Katharine and her works at:
www.katharinehamilton.com

Social Media is a great way to connect with Katharine. Check her out on the following:

Facebook: Katharine E. Hamilton
https://www.facebook.com/Katharine-E-Hamilton-282475125097433/

Twitter: @AuthorKatharine
Instagram: @AuthorKatharine

Contact Katharine:
khamiltonauthor@gmail.com

ABOUT THE AUTHOR

Katharine E. Hamilton began writing in 2008 and published her first children's book, The Adventurous Life of Laura Bell in 2009. She would go on to write and illustrate two more children's books, Susie At Your Service and Sissy and Kat between 2010-2013.

Though writing for children was fun, Katharine moved into Adult Fiction in 2015 with her release of The Unfading Lands, a clean, epic fantasy that landed in Amazon's Hot 100 New Releases on its fourth day of publication, reached #72 in the Top 100 in Epic Fantasy, and hit the Top 10,000 Best Sellers on all of Amazon in its first week. It has been listed as a Top 100 Indie Read for 2015 and a nominee for a Best Indie Book Award for 2016. The series did not stop there. Darkness Divided: Part Two of The Unfading Land Series, released in October of 2015 and claimed a spot in the Top 100 of its genre. Redemption Rising: Part Three of The Unfading Lands Series released in April 2016 and claimed a nomination for the Summer Indie Book Awards.

Though comfortable in the fantasy genre, Katharine decided to venture towards romance in 2017 and released the first novel in a collection of sweet, clean and wholesome romances: The Lighthearted Collection. Chicago's Best reached best seller status in its first week of publication and rested comfortably in the Top 100 for Amazon for three steady weeks, claimed a Reader's Choice Award, a TopShelf Indie Book Award, and ended up a finalist in the American Book Festival's

Best Book Awards for 2017. <u>Montgomery House</u>, the second in the collection, released in August of 2017 and rested comfortably alongside its predecessor, claiming a Reader's Choice Award, and becoming Katharine's best-selling novel up to that point. Both were released in audiobook format in late 2017 and early 2018. <u>Beautiful Fury</u> is the third novel released in the collection and has claimed a Reader's Choice Award and a gold medal in the Authorsdb Best Cover competition. It has also been released in audiobook format with narrator Chelsea Carpenter lending her talents to bring it to life. Katharine and Chelsea have partnered on an ongoing project for creating audiobook marketing methods for fellow authors and narrators, all of which will eventually be published as a resource tool for others.

In August of 2018, Katharine brought to life a new clean contemporary romance series of a loving family based in Ireland. The Siblings O'Rifcan Series kicked off in August with <u>Claron</u>. <u>Claron</u> climbed to the Top 1000 of the entire Amazon store and has reached the Top 100 of the Clean and Wholesome genre a total of 11 times. He is Katharine's bestselling book thus far and lends to the success of the following books in the series: <u>Riley</u>, <u>Layla</u>, <u>Chloe</u>, and <u>Murphy,</u> each book earning their place in the Top 100 of their genre and Hot 100 New Releases. <u>Claron</u> was featured in Amazon's Prime Reading program March – June 2019. The series is also available in audiobook format with the voice talents of Alex Black.

A Love For All Seasons, a Sweet Contemporary Romance Series launched in July of 2019 with

Summer's Catch, followed by Autumn's Fall in October. Winter's Call and Spring's Hope scheduled for 2021 release dates. The series follows a wonderful group of friends from Friday Harbor, Washington, and has been Katharine's newest and latest project.

Graham, Book One in The Brothers of Hastings Ranch Series launched a new collection of stories in the Clean and Wholesome and Western Romance genres of Amazon for Katharine. All books have reached best seller status and continue to hold their places with enthusiasm.

Katharine has contributed to charitable Indie Anthologies as well as helped other aspiring writers journey their way through the publication process. She manages an online training course that walks fellow self-publishing and independently publishing writers through the publishing process as well as how to market their books.

She is a member of Women Fiction Writers of America, Texas Authors, IASD, and the American Christian Fiction Writers. She loves everything to do with writing and loves that she is able to continue sharing heartwarming stories to a wide array of readers.

Katharine graduated from Texas A&M University with a bachelor's degree in History. She lives on the coast of Texas with her husband Brad, sons Everett and West, and their two dogs, Tulip and Paws.

Printed in Great Britain
by Amazon